# MAR'

## Introduction

A fictional amble through a not so typical family life.

The story revolves around the main character Mary, with several twists, turns and complications along the way.

Tony her long term discreet romance, Whom she thought she'd met twenty five years ago, provides the first quirk in the story.

Mary's husband, Thomas went missing somewhere in Asia, assumed killed in 1983, but his past life continues to create serious disruptions for Mary and her family.

The story begins in 2007 with the wedding of Mary's daughter Gillian, and and extends over the following decade.

Printed in larger text for easier reading

The story and characters are totally fictional and similarity to real life is purely coincidental

## Chapter One

The headlights illuminated the narrow drive access between the sturdy brick piers as Mary carefully positioned her fourteen year old silver Mercedes within a couple of feet of the garage door. Much too tired to bother garaging the vehicle, she collected her evening bag and quietly closed the driver's door. As she emerged from the shadow of the garage, her four bedroom property and the surrounding area became flooded with light from the newly installed security system.

Mary quickly unlocked and entered through her front door. Once inside she kicked off her shoes and hastily went into the kitchen, switching on the lights on the way. She looked back at the partly glazed front door to see the outside return to darkness. "Thank goodness" she muttered to herself, imagining what her awakened neighbours must be thinking at this unearthly hour of the night. Although feeling worn out and exhausted from dancing all evening she still couldn't resist the urge to practice a few rumba steps on the smooth tiled kitchen floor while waiting for her milk to warm in the microwave.

Relying on the moonlight to find her

way around her bedroom, she placed the mug of warm sweetened milk on to the bedside table. As she sat propped up in bed she could look through the side of the bay window towards the sea front. Watching the moon glistening on the water and feeling unable to get to sleep, her thoughts returned to recollect that she had earlier in that day walked her lovely daughter Gillian down the aisle to be married.

Mary took on this roll as her husband Thomas, a foreign correspondent working at the time for a daily national newspaper had been reported missing somewhere in Asia in nineteen eighty three, twenty four years ago, assumed killed.

The wedding had gone perfectly, her son, also Thomas, the grooms best friend was the best man with two of Gillian's teacher school friends as her bridesmaids.

The reception at the Oakland Hall Hotel just off the sea front for the congregation of about forty guests was followed by a buffet and dance in the evening in the hotel ballroom, with the music provided by an accomplished trio comprising of two very smartly dressed young men, one playing a keyboard and the other a set of drums, accompanied by a more mature attractive lady vocalist.

The evening was attended by a further

twenty or so of the couple's friends and their partners. The musicians carefully calculated the music to suit the differing age groups.

Although Tony her long time friend, was Mary's dance partner, there were several other able gentlemen eagerly waiting their chance to waltz this slim elegant good looking lady around the floor.

For the last half hour of the evening Mary had slumped into one of the chairs surrounding the floor before collecting her grey and cream checked costume jacket from the cloakroom. On returning to the ballroom in order to say her 'good nights', "Now is the hour". Sweetly sang the lady vocalist. Almost immediately with her jacket over one arm, Tony appeared and danced Mary around the floor to the last waltz.

As the guests began to leave, Gillian Hines, nee Hooper and Robert Stewart Hines, the proud newly wedded couple stood in the doorway and embraced and thanked everyone in turn. Mary thought to herself. 'That was a wonderful day'.

Sunday morning arrived for Mary about half past ten as the bright warm sunlight streamed through the windows, eventually dazzling her closed eyes. Slowly she reached to lift the ornate silver framed photograph of her then forty years old husband Thomas, wondering what he would look like on this day if he was still alive.

She carefully placed it next to the matching framed picture of her three children, Thomas Daniel and Gillian as she eased her feet onto the carpeted floor.

As Mary approached the front door to collect the local 'Cornish Journal' and gather up the loose material that had spilled from out of the newspaper on to the floor, she became aware of a figure the other side of the door. Tony grinned as the door was opened.

"What on earth are you doing round here ?" Mary asked, totally bemused by his unexpected presence.

"I just wanted to see you, I thought we could go out for lunch, that's if you want to". Tony replied.

"Well, if you insist, it'll save me the bother of cooking tonight. I'll just make us some coffee".

"What's this ?" Tony called out from the lounge, referring to an overstuffed ledger type of book. Bound with flowery wallpaper pasted to the original hard cover, looking very tatty and hanging loose in places, all tied up with a broad yellow ribbon.

"Oh.....put that down, don't you dare open it. That's my scrapbook, I started it when I was a kid, some of it's very childish. And personal". Mary said as she swiftly approached the lounge to prevent Tony from doing exactly what Mary knew he would do. "I was feeling a bit nostalgic this morning after seeing Gillian get married. My wedding album's on the sideboard, you can have a look through that".

"This is the first time you've ever shown me your wedding photos". Tony quipped as he settled down on the settee. Mary unceremoniously plonked his drink on the coffee table a couple of feet away from him. "He was a handsome bloke, your Thomas. You look absolutely stunning, now let's have a peep at this scrapbook". Tony chirped as he retrieved the heavy item from the floor at his feet.

"I'll do it". Mary snapped and wrestled the book from Tony's grip. "You can start looking from here". She added as she parted the book leaving almost a third of the pages secret. "They're all my school days stuff, you don't want to see any of that".

For the moment Tony patiently accepted Mary's decision and listened intently to her comments and description of the various items she had accumulated and why she had stuck them in the album.

"That's a cutting from a newspaper of

mum and dad when they won some local ballroom dance competition, and this one's of my sister Susan, she won the junior cup for ballroom on the same night. You danced with her a couple of times last night...I saw you, you couldn't take your eyes off her". Mary moaned.

"Is she still here ?" Tony enquired hopefully.

"No, they've gone by now, they came down in a camper van and gone off touring Cornwall. They are coming down again at the beginning of September to stay with me". Mary answered. "Anyway this is all boring stuff for you. Close it up and drink your coffee, it's going cold".

"Come on......let me see your school stuff, it can't be that bad". Tony laughed.

"Oh alright, but I'll hold on to the book". Mary insisted. Tony started a smile which quickly turned into a laugh as he began to read what appeared to be a schoolboy love letter from a lad named Bernard. "Was he your first boyfriend then ?" Tony asked and proceeded to read the letter out loud.

"Stop making fun of me, he was just a boy who had a crush on me. We were only eleven, I went out with him once, we just went to the park and walked round with his dog". Mary attempted to force the book closed, but Tony resisted and began reading one of Mary's school reports.

"My God, you had top marks in every subject but I do like the comment in the teacher's assessment box. "Mary is a very remarkable pupil and should be very proud of her results, but she does posses a cheeky streak and often disrupts the class".

"That's it......let me close the book". Mary screeched at the same time unable to contain her own laughter.

"Okay, but let me have a look at the photos I nearly managed to see, looks like your holiday snaps when you were young". Tony pestered.

Mary reluctantly reopened the album and together they looked and commented on several family seaside pictures. "This is when I met Thomas. This was the first time me and Susan were allowed to go away on our own. We went to...."

"Swanage !!" Tony butted in excitedly, and that lad there is me !!!" He blurted out. "It's bloody well me, oh my God. It is me". He repeated assertively.

"Oh sod off, stop playing the fool. This was in nineteen fifty eight". Mary scoffed dismissively. "Come on then idiot...which one is you ?" She added, wondering which boy he would point to.

"Him, that's me". Tony shouted, unable

to control the volume of his voice.

"Me and that other chap were on our bikes, we were staying at the youth hostel up that very steep hill. That's not Susan, the girl in this photo with me?"

"Yes. That is my sister, but it's not you. You're having me on!" Mary replied, now beginning to get slightly irritated by Tony's insistence.

"Tell me, were the two lads in this photo on a biking holiday?" Tony asked impatiently. Mary hesitated and wondered how Tony could know this. 'I've never talked about this holiday before, so how does he know this?' She thought.

"Honestly….it is me". Tony pleaded convincingly. "I remember we followed you and your sister from out of the amusements and round on to the end of the pier, then you began to chat with us. Now do you believe me?" Mary slumped back into the settee and just stared at Tony totally bewildered by what she'd just come to accept.

"Oh my God…….and I married your mate!"

"Well you married the other chap but he wasn't my mate. We only met the day before at the Bridport YHA and it was only because we were both going to go on to Swanage that we got together. We had three nights in Swanage and after we left you two girls I went on to Gosport and I think he set off back home". Mary let out another couple of 'Oh Gods' before putting her arms round Tony's neck and gave him a passionate kiss.

"I must ring Susan, she's never going to believe it". Mary gushed excitedly.

"You said she's coming down in September, it's only a few weeks away, let's wait till then and show her the pictures and see her face". Tony suggested as Mary held the telephone poised to make the call.

"I don't know if I can hold out that long without saying anything, she rings me every week. I'm bound to cave in". Mary replied and dropped herself back on the settee. Nursing the album on her lap she gazed with tearful eyes at the photographs of Tony cuddling with her sister Susan as they sat together on the sea wall. "Why didn't you pick me ?" She cried.

"I thought we were going out to lunch". Tony interjected to bring Mary back from the year nineteen fifty eight.

"Yes, we are". Mary replied lovingly. She reached across, placing the scrapbook onto the coffee table open to the page displaying the black and white holiday snaps. "Why didn't you pick me fifty years ago ?" She repeated pitifully as Tony held both her hands and lifted her to her feet.

Late that evening after Tony had left for his own home about eight miles east, towards Plymouth, Mary carefully lifted the fragile scrapbook and opened it to a page beyond the point she'd allowed Tony to see. "Now then". She said to herself as she bypassed the last used page to attach several details of her daughter's wedding, including an invitation card and a copy of the reception menu. The previous page drew her attention, being a brief family history she had noted some years ago with the dream of writing a novel, which never materialised due to her inability to imagine a story to weave into her family characters. "I can add all the information about Tony now, that might give me the start of a plot". She said out loud, again talking to herself, but not having a pen to hand she decided. "I'll do that tomorrow". Turning back to the previous page. "Now what did I actually write". Mary delved between the cushions to retrieve her reading glasses.

*Notes…ideas for my book. Title ????*

*Mary Dawson was born in 1942 in a tiny village a few miles from Warwick. She met her husband Thomas Hooper when they were both sixteen years old while on a* holiday in Dorset with her older sister Susan. Thomas lived in Plymouth so Mary was very surprised when he turned up on her doorstep a couple of weeks later. He stayed with a relative of his in Birmingham and eventually secured a job in that city with a local evening newspaper. And in 1961 after a three year long courtship, at the very young age of 19 they were married in Mary's village church. By now Mary had completed her extra years at college and they made the decision to return to live in Thomas's home town, where they rented a two bedroom flat. Thomas their first child was born in 1971. By now, both having very well paid occupations, Thomas a journalist and Mary a chief librarian, they were able to take out a mortgage on a house of their own. This took them twenty miles west to a small Cornish seaside town, the four bedroom property where Mary still lives. Two years later Daniel was born and with Thomas now spending more time in foreign countries Mary was forced to give up her career to care for her two young children. She was however fortunate to have the help of a friendly neighbour to look after her children for one whole day each week. This allowed her a brief social life, albeit just a visit to the local tea dance. On Jan. 3rd. 1983 Mary *waved goodbye to her husband as his train departed from Plymouth en route to London, little knowing that this would be the last time she would ever see him. He'd been home for Christmas after a four month assignment in South Africa and was now being posted to Lebanon in Asia. He was last reported as leaving Beirut on a military vehicle on the 6th of Feb. These dates now firmly embedded in Mary's mind. Mary's third child, Gillian was born later in the year without Thomas knowing she ever existed. The previous year at a tea dance on Mary's 40th birthday she first met Anthony Pennel and the two have remained the very best of friends ever since.*

'That's enough to bore anyone'. Mary thought as she deliberated as to whether to visit the desk in the hallway for a biro and add details about Tony, but now thoroughly tired she closed the scrapbook and went up to bed.

+++++++++++

## Chapter Two

The warm sunshine greeted Mary as she closed her front door on this pleasant Monday morning in late July. Wearing only a printed blue and cream cotton dress, she strolled the hundred yards or so from her house to the promenade and crossed the road and carefully lowered herself down the two foot drop onto the sandy beach. Putting on her dark sunglasses to shield her eyes from the glare, and with the ebbing tide gently lapping the shore, Mary set off on the smooth firm sand at the water's edge to walk the mile journey to the town centre.

After a leisurely fifteen minute stroll, weaving in and out of several family groups playing on the beach, Mary hopped up the wooden set of steps back on to the promenade. Balancing on one leg in turn she removed the sand from her sandals. A lull in the busy shore road traffic allowed Mary to safely cross to the opposite pavement and enter through the open door of the small corner shop owned by her son Daniel and his wife Debra.

The shop although minimal in size has been cleverly laid out in aisles as a mini market selling a limited range of food goods. The store also acts as a news agents whilst also catering for holiday visitors beach requirements.

As Debra was busy attending to a queue of customers Mary wandered to the rear of the store to the newspaper section. After browsing the headlines of several daily papers she selected a couple of ladies magazines together with her usual paper. With her chosen reading material Mary tagged on to the queue behind the remaining two young attractive lady customers who appeared to be together. Mary assumed as they were both dressed suitably for the beach in coloured shorts, bikini tops and flip flops, and by their strong Welsh accents, they were most certainly on holiday.

Debra was still not aware of her mother-in-law's presence as she chatted and shared a joke with the holiday couple. "Do you both still live in Wales ?" Debra asked as she handed one lady the change.

"Oh yes.....I live in Bridgend and she's my sister, and she lives in Swansea. We came down last Saturday for a fortnight, we're up at the caravan park. Suppose our little break's over, let's get back to see how our other halves are coping with the kids". The eldest looking lady commented.

"The beach is pretty crowded, we could just pretend we couldn't find them and bugger off for the rest of the morning". Her sister joked in her strong accent.

"Oh.....I never saw you there Mary". Debra called out. "Enjoy the rest of your holiday". She remarked to the Welsh ladies as they left the shop laughing hysterically.

"They're a pleasant couple". Mary commented and placed her papers on the counter with one hand while holding several photographs in the other, splayed out like a poker hand in cards.

"I wish all my customers were like that, we do get some real awkward devils in here at times. Anyway Mary you look as if you're dying to show me something. What's with the photos, are they Gillian's wedding ?"

"No. Who would you say that lad is in these holiday snaps". Mary gushed, bubbling with excitement, spreading the pictures on the counter..

Before Debra had chance to look Mary let out an excited loud squeal. "That's Tony !" And launched into a rapid incoherent dialogue.

"Slow down Mary, what are you talking about. Why all the excitement about Tony's childhood photos. They look like his seaside holiday snaps". Debra said calmly.

"They're not any of Tony's photos, they're mine from one of my holidays with Susan. It's the holiday when I met Thomas when I was sixteen. Tony is the other lad with Susan".

Debra stared unconvincingly at the black and white photographs. "What on earth makes you think that ? Has Tony been kidding you on again ?"

Throughout the following hour, and punctuated by several interruptions allowing for Debra to serve her customers, eventually being convinced by Mary's explanation, Debra finally accepted that Tony was the other lad. "Oh my God, it's unbelievable, and all this time he's been wanting to marry you. Have you told Susan and Gillian and the lads yet ? I can't wait to tell Daniel when he gets back". Debra chuckled.

"I tried Gillian and Thomas before I came out, but neither of them answered. I'll ring them again when I get home. We're not going to tell Susan, she's coming down for a couple of weeks soon. We want to see her face when she finds out". Mary replied. "And they actually danced together at the wedding. That's amazing". Mary added

"Changing the subject, what did you think of the wedding ?" Mary asked.

"Wonderful, and to think I actually got Daniel on the dance floor, thanks to those lessons you and Tony gave us. He's even talking about going to dance classes".

"Well why not, Tony never regretted it. We would never had met.....met again !... .if

18

he hadn't learnt to dance, and we would never have known anything about these photos". Mary quipped.

"They're off on their honeymoon this morning, Robert's mum and his uncle are dropping them off at Southampton on their way home. My.....a Caribbean cruise, no messing with newly weds these days, we had a week in Torquay in a holiday flat, self catering !" Mary added.

"I thought Thomas made a great speech, bit cheeky mind. How long has he known Robert ?" Debra asked.

"Oh, since Robert was sixteen he was working up at the holiday camp and he went along for a trial at Thomas's club. It was Thomas who got him his first date with our Gillian".

"Anyway I must go you've got some customers wanting to be served, I'm just popping into town for a look round". Mary left the cool of the shop as she stepped around a young mum and her two children busily choosing from the array of beach items from the many containers situated at the back of the pavement set against the shop front and continued her walk in the hot midday sunshine.

After a modest purchase of a light lunch and a smart fashionable sun hat from the indoor shopping mall, now refreshed and with the hat sitting stylishly on her head, she crossed back to the sea front for the return stroll home along the promenade.

In the cool of her lounge, with the sun now having moved round to the west, Mary relaxed with a cup of tea, and then after spending another frustrating couple of hours on the telephone trying with great difficulty, and obviously without the benefit of showing the photographs, to convince Thomas and his wife Elaine about Tony and the Swanage holiday. She slumped full length onto the settee, closed her eyes and let her mind re-visit the wedding and how Gillian came to meet Robert.

Robert worked at the nearby caravan park at the time and arrived one Saturday lunchtime with her eldest son Thomas on the way to play football. Gillian and Robert just said hello and they smiled pleasantly at each other on meeting.

The shy handsome sixteen year old lad obviously liked her, as that same evening after the match, Thomas telephoned her at Robert's request. They met later that night outside the local cinema and have been together ever since.

When the holiday season ended Robert and his friend from the camp rented a flat nearby. Robert then enrolled in a teacher training college for a couple of years and eventually secured a position at the local boys senior school. Later due to his sporting ability, when offered he chose to become head of sport.

Robert and his mother endured a hostile environment with his father throughout most of his childhood. As soon as he left school he came to work and live in Cornwall and shortly afterwards without any warning his father walked out of the family home and to his mother's relief he never returned or made contact again.

Lightening entering the bedroom through open curtains in the early hours of the morning failed to awaken Mary. With the distant rumbling of thunder gradually getting closer, and with the strong wind driving the rain hard against the windows it seemed that the current heat wave had come to an end. Eventually a very loud crack of thunder startled Mary from her deep sleep. The next flash of lightening lit up the photographs on the bedside table. She now felt quite vulnerable all alone in the house she once shared with her husband and their children. Mary approached the side bay window, and in the light created by each flash of lightening she watched the surf spewing onto the promenade.

Returning to sit on the edge of the bed she stared at the framed photograph of Thomas, recalling the last day he was seen and what horror he may have endured. Unable to prevent the tears running down her cheeks and with the dawn light brightening the room, she lifted herself back into bed and turned away from the picture in the hope of another couple hours of sleep.

+++++++++++

## Chapter Three

Mary stared from her open front door, watching Tony wiping a smudge from the roof of his new Mercedes with the sleeve of his smart pale grey suit jacket.

"So you got it then....copy cat!" Mary joked. "I see you bought the Merc then". She added as she reached the garden wall.

"Well.....do you like it, what do you think?" Tony asked, expecting another wise crack from Mary.

"It's very nice, I love the pale blue colour. I'm banning it from the drive, it will show mine up". Mary replied with a chuckle as she wandered all round the shiny vehicle. "And....come on, how much did you pay for it?"

"Thirty five". Tony hesitantly replied.

"Struth! I assume you got a full tank of petrol in that deal".

"It wasn't too bad, the fella' allowed me fifteen hundred for my Mazda". Tony quipped. "It is only three months old, and a brand new S class is twice that".

"I'm only winding you up, it is a beautiful car, come on let's get going".

Mary fastened her seat belt and Tony carefully drove the short distance to the sea front and eastward along the shore road.

"Before I forget, your Tom gave me a photo he took at the wedding, it's on the back seat, he thought you might like to take it if you still intend visiting your mum next weekend".

"No, I've decided not to go. If I go I'd have to call on Susan, and I'd have to tell her about you. So what I thought, after she's had her holiday with me I might drive her back home and see mum then".

After a twenty minute drive the smart gleaming Mercedes entered the large hotel car park. Tony drove slowly passed several vacant spaces to leave his vehicle parked up safely in the furthermost isolated space possible.

"Tony, for goodness sake go a bit closer, there's no bus running from here. You'll have to hang on a minute, I need to change, I'll ruin my new dance shoes by the time we've walked to the hotel through all these puddles".

"You shouldn't be walking outside in your dance shoes anyway". Tony replied as he held an open umbrella to protect Mary.

The couple entered through the hotel reception and on into the modest size function room used for the Tuesday tea dance.

The melodious sound of 'Moon River'

was being played on the keyboard with several couples gracefully gliding around the floor to tempo of the waltz.

"Hello you two, not usual for you not to be here at the start, I wondered if you were going to miss a dance". Les the key board musician remarked as he tinkled off the last few bars.

"We'd never not turn up Les, It's Tony's fault. He's just bought himself a new car and we've had to spend some time admiring it". Mary replied sarcastically.

"What you gone and bought then Tone ?" Les asked enthusiastically.

"Mercedes three fifty S class". Tony stuttered embarrassingly. "It's only a few months old so it'll see me out".

"Wow, I'll have a gander before you leave". Les exclaimed as he handed Tony some change.

Tony and Mary reached their customary table on the far side of the floor.

"Take your partners for a quickstep". Les announced as he began to play the music.

"Oh, by the way, I almost forgot, Gillian phoned just before you distracted me with your car. They had just got to their cabin. You never told me you'd upgraded their cabin. Gillian was hysterical with excitement. She told me to give you a big kiss from her. She said they're on the top deck with a private balcony". Mary retorted with grateful admiration for Tony's thoughtfulness.

"Call it an extra wedding present". Tony responded.

"Yes, I know you think the world of Gillian, it must have been a wonderful surprise for them. Why didn't you tell me you'd done that ?" Mary replied.

"I didn't tell you, because you're as bad as Gillian, it wouldn't have been a secret for long, you wouldn't have been able to resist telling her".

Mary jumped in sharply. "While we're on the subject of secrets, Gillian made me promise not to let you know she'd told me, so don't go saying anything. She told me that you'd given them the money for the deposit on their cottage. Why did you keep that from me ?"

"I thought you might consider that I was interfering too much if you had known about it". Tony explained. "We'd better have a dance". He added lifting Mary to her feet.

"No I think it was lovely and very generous of you, you have every right to help her. I know how much you've missed over the years". Mary gushed with admiration for Tony as they danced around the floor to a foxtrot.

"There's a few strange faces in here today". Tony commented as Les arrived at their table on his normal interval stroll to greet everyone.

"Yes Tone, it's probably down to the weather, Those three couples are here on holiday, they're staying in the hotel". Les murmured as he discreetly pointed to a table in the far corner of the room. "I'd better wander on".

After a complete circuit of the floor, Les stood by the small raised stage, one hand resting on the edge of his keyboard while drinking from a cup with the other. "Ready to go again folks ?" He called out and began playing the music for the next dance.

"You all on your own today young Ted ?" Tony remarked as several couples were leaving. "Yes". The lively eighty six year old replied. "Kate's got her grand kids and her daughter staying with her on holiday, she'll be back next week. Had me leg loose today, I spread myself around a bit". "Yes we did notice, lucky ladies". Mary added with a laugh.

After a few brief pauses across the car park to allow the Mercedes to be admired, and a scheduled stop right in front of the hotel entrance to oblige Les, Tony began the return journey.

"Don't forget your photograph". Tony reminded Mary as she closed the front passenger door. "It's under my newspaper".

"That's lovely, he's put it in a frame for me". Mary announced as she stretched across the rear seats.

"Gillian looks beautiful, just like mum". Tony flattered sincerely.

Tony made one more circuit of his car before smartly striding up the path to join Mary in the kitchen.

"I'll make a cup of coffee, but don't get changing into your grunge, we're eating out tonight, I've booked a table at the Italiano for half seven". Mary asserted.

"When did you organise that ? And what's the occasion ?" Tony asked.

"I made the call at the dance when you went to the toilets. It's just to say thank you for all the things you've done for Gillian". Mary answered sweetly. "We both know why". She whispered.

+++++++++++

# Chapter Four

Mary dashed into the lounge and lifted the receiver anticipating a call from her daughter. "Oh it's you Susan". Mary grunted.

"Don't seem so pleased to hear from me, sorry to disappoint you". Susan joked. "Is it all right if I come down to you on Monday. That's this Monday the third ?"

"That's the day after tomorrow". Mary answered.

"Yes, sorry for dropping it on you at such short notice, I can leave it to another week if it's any problem". Susan said apologetically.

"No, it's no problem, just took me unawares that's all. That'll be great". Mary confirmed.

"It's only me, I'm coming on the National, I hate to ask but it only goes as far as Plymouth". Susan paused as Mary interrupted.

"No Walter ? Of course I'll meet you at the bus station, what time do you get in ?"

"Walter intended to come and we would have come in the car, but he finally got himself a job last week and he doesn't want to have to ask for time off already. Its supposed to get to Plymouth at five".

"Okay I'll be there, if there's any change

let me know". Mary retorted.

"Will that gorgeous fella' of yours be with you". Susan asked cheekily, almost prompting Mary to spoil the secret.

"I dare say he'll want to come along. See you Monday then, somethings burning in the kitchen, have to go. Bye". Mary ended the conversation abruptly before the temptation became too great. 'Damn, I forgot to tell her Gillian and Robert get home on Tuesday'.

Mary waved frantically the moment she spotted Susan sitting on her suitcase in the coach terminal and watched as Tony strode swiftly across the tarmac, and looked on slightly enviously as he greeted her with a hug and a kiss on the cheek. Having had time to think about the implications of the secret they were about to reveal.

"Why do you two keep looking at each other and grinning, is my skirt tucked in my knickers, or something ?" Susan quipped after they'd travelled a couple of miles. "This isn't your car Mary ?"

"No....it's Tony's, he's only had it few weeks. It looks a bit like mine". Mary said and burst out laughing, "We've got to tell her". She blurted out, unable to contain herself.

"Come on tell me what ? I know there's

something going on". Susan snapped.

"Wait till we get to Mary's, you're in for a big surprise". Tony chipped in, giving Mary a stern look and a sideways shake of his head.

"Oh come on, tell me now". Susan pleaded.

"We're nearly there now, only another ten minutes. it'll be worth the wait".

"Okay, no more messing me about, what have I done that's so funny ?" Susan angrily demanded to know the second Mary opened her front door.

"Go in the lounge and have a look at those holiday snaps on the coffee table". Mary instructed.

"So..!" Susan exclaimed. "They're our holiday in Swanage in nineteen fifty eight. I've got these pictures myself. What am I supposed to be looking at ?"

"Who do you think that lad is with his arm round you ?" Tony asked excitedly.

"I don't know, I can't remember his name. Who do you think he is ?"

"It's Tony !" Mary screeched beating Tony to the announcement.

"Go away, is this what all the grinning was about. You're having me on". Susan replied, now getting very irritated at the thought of being the butt of a practical joke.

"It's true". Tony said forcefully and then spent the next hour telling Susan stories about the three days they spent together which only that lad would know.

"I remember I gave you my address and you promised to write to me". Susan quipped having been convinced it was Tony.

"I did intend to, but I couldn't find that piece of paper you gave me when I got home, so I never did"..... "sorry". Tony apologised with a sigh.

Mary felt twinges of jealousy at being left out of this reunion. "I'll put the kettle on". She uttered, and left Tony and her sister in a huddle on the settee.

"I'm not going to the tea dance today". Mary stated. "You still go with Tony, Gillian just phoned, they've just docked, so I'll be going to Plymouth again to pick them up when their train gets in".

"That's if Tony will want to go without you". Susan replied hopefully.

"I'm sure he will, go and get ready, he'll be here at two".

Mary stared with admiration at her sister wearing a simple low cut pale green dress, the top half tightly fitting with the flared skirt to just below the knee.

"Wow....you look stunning. I just hope the old fellas' at the dance have had their pacemakers charged up".

"This thing with Tony, surely he already knew it was Swanage when he shouted out. You must have told him that's where you met Thomas". Susan uttered.

"No, I'd told him we met on holiday but I didn't say where, and he never met Thomas". Mary responded. "Anyway he's here, he's at the door" She added.

"I'll let him in". Susan gushed excitedly

"Oh my.....I love your dress'. Tony gulped. "Susan is coming with us ?".

"I've told her to get back up those stairs and get dressed". Mary joked.

"I'm staying here. Gillian phoned to tell me they had just docked. So I'm just waiting now for her let me know what time they'll be back so that I can pick them up. But Susan's all ready so you go with Susan, she's dying to go dancing, she never gets a chance at home". Mary said wondering if it was the wisest suggestion she'd ever made.

"I'll leave you some dinner in the oven". Mary advised as Tony and Susan left for the dance.

The telephone had been ringing for almost a minute before Mary realised and came in from the garden.

"Hello Gillian, you on your way ?" Mary

assumed, fully expecting her daughter to give her the time of their arrival at Plymouth station. "What's the matter you sound a bit upset, are you alright ?"

"Robert's mum has had an accident, his uncle met us off the boat and he's taking Robert to the hospital".

"What happened to her ? Is she badly hurt ?" Mary asked anxiously.

"I don't know, but she's in a coma, his uncle Ron said it only happened late yesterday afternoon. She fainted or had a seizure and fell getting off the bus".

"Oh my God, I hope she's going to be alright. How long is it going to take you to get to the hospital ?"

"I'm not with them mum. I'm stood here on Southampton station waiting for my train. I could have gone with them but I wanted to get home, They dropped me off and sorted me out with a ticket, but I've no idea what time the next train is, I'll have to pop back to the booking office and find out. I'll ring you back and let you know".

"Ring me as soon as you can Gillian. I'll pick you up, let me know the time it gets in". By the time Mary had closed the French doors to the garden and started to prepare the evening meal the telephone rang again. "Yes Gillian". Mary answered, patiently. "Did you find out the time ?"

"The next train doesn't leave here until twenty five past three and gets into Plymouth about half past six". Gillian replied.

"Okay Gillian, I'll be there to meet you. You've got a couple of hours to kill, go and get yourself something to eat".

"I'll let you know if Robert rings me, in any case I'll ring you again from the train when it's nearer to Plymouth. Bye for now mum".

"It looks as though Mary's still here". Tony said to Susan, seeing the Mercedes on the drive as they returned from the dance. "Is their train delayed ?". Tony asked as Mary opened the door.

"No, it's Robert's mum". Mary said and then began to explain the circumstances. "Gillian gets into Plymouth at half six so I'm going to be away in half an hour. I've cooked your dinners, they're in the oven keeping warm".

"Give me ten minutes to eat and I'll run you to the station". Tony offered.

"Okay that's great, are you coming with us Susan ?" Mary asked.

"I think I'll stay here, I'm absolutely shattered after the dance and yesterday's journey. You two get off, leave everything, I'll clean up here".

"Did Susan enjoy the dance ?" Mary asked as soon as she was alone in the car with Tony.

"Well she wore me out, insisted on doing every dance. If I hesitated she was off with someone else. Yes I think you could say she enjoyed it. My.....can she dance". Tony replied. "She was certainly the bell of the ball. Eyes on sticks most of them".

"No one had a coronary then". Mary chirped.

"I almost did, I'm bloody exhausted. Anyway we're here now, you go on to the platform, I'll get a car parking ticket and join you in a minute".

Tony arrived at Mary's side slightly the worse for wear just as the train drew into the station, doors began to spring open. Mary scoured the length of the platform watching commuters leaving and boarding the train.

"There she is.....there's Gillian". Tony announced, seeing her down at the far end, looking a very lonely figure standing by her luggage on the almost deserted platform with the Penzance train now departed.

First Mary then Tony gave Gillian a hug as she raced to join them, leaving a couple of bags unattended. Tony quickly strode the fifty yards and returned dragging the wheeled items behind him.

---

"You've not heard any more about Robert's mum ?" Tony asked after having an additional hug and a kiss from Gillian causing him to release the luggage. "What was that for ?"

"That was from me and Robert for that wonderful surprise of the cabin upgrade".

"It was my pleasure, as long as you had a good time, that's all that counts". Tony replied, basking in the affection from Gillian.

Mary repeated Tony's earlier question. "Has Robert rung you ?

"Yes, I was just going to tell you. They went straight to the hospital, she's in Guildford. He said he'd just seen her and she is conscious. He said she's got some bad cuts and bruises and still seems to be in a daze. She can't remember what she did, she couldn't remember falling from the bus. The hospital intend to keep her in for the rest of the week for tests to try and find the cause for her seizure".

"What's Robert going to do now ?" Mary enquired.

"He's going to stay at his mum's for a few days. He says it's not too far away, it's in Woking ". Gillian replied. "She's got an old people's bungalow. It used to be his gran's. After his dad vanished his mum had no way of paying the mortgage on their house so the building society repossessed it. His gran died three years ago but they allowed his mum to carry on living there".

"She hasn't had an easy life, has she? How old is Robert's mum?" Mary asked.

"She's only sixty, she was only fifty seven when his gran died and she expected to be made homeless. She's happy there and got lots of friends".

"I'll sit in the back with Gillian". Mary said, dropping the armrest down between them. "So you enjoyed yourselves then".

"Oh mum it was fantastic. You and Tony will have to go on a cruise for your honeymoon". Gillian quipped and began to giggle.

"Tony made eye contact in the driver mirror with Mary and grinned. "You cheeky little bugger". Mary scoffed and burst into laughter.

"Oh my God, in all the confusion I completely forgot to tell you…..your auntie Susan is staying with me, she came down yesterday". Mary exclaimed. "Your junction is soon, would you like to come and stay with us until Robert gets back?"

"I'd like to go home mum, the cottage has been empty for nearly a month now, I'm looking forward to seeing it again. I will come round sometime tomorrow to see aunt Susan". Gillian replied apologetically.

"Well come round for lunch". Mary insisted.

Gillian and Robert have lived in their end of terrace two bedroom, two story cottage in a small village some six miles inland from Mary for nearly three years.

Gillian and Robert got married in the pretty village church, Gillian chose to walk the short distance from home attended by her two bridesmaids supporting the dress and train. Fortunately the weather forecast was totally wrong and the day turned out to be glorious.

The Mercedes left the busy main road for the solitude of the quiet country lanes for last few miles. Passing the local stores, Tony travelled a further three hundred yards to arrive outside Gillian's cottage.

Gillian's good friend and neighbour appeared from the adjoining cottage, but before she managed to ask, Gillian hastily explained why Robert was missing. "This is Maxine from next door, she's been looking after the house for us".

"Yes we know Maxine, we met at the wedding, me and Maxine had a waltz". Tony chirped. "Yes we did, it's lovely to see you again". Maxine quipped.

"We'll just see you settled in and we'll be off". Mary said. Tony clattered the tiny front door as he lifted the heavy bags over the threshold. "What you got in here Gillian, the ship's anchor ?" Tony joked.

"That's all my stuff, Robert must have it in his". Gillian shouted from the kitchen. "Do you want a cup of tea before you go ?" Gillian shouted again.

"No....you get yourself sorted out and I'll see you tomorrow, I've got a fantastic surprise to tell you". Mary replied leaving her daughter wanting more information.

"She's certainly one gorgeous young lady, just like her mother". Tony remarked admiringly observing Gillian through the car rear view mirror.

"Are you going to come in for a while ?" Mary asked as the car drew up to her house.

"It's getting a bit late, I'll get on. You and Susan can have an evening together".

The sound of the key inserted in the front door startled Susan from her brief nap in the armchair. "Sorry, did I wake you ?"

"I must have just dozed off". Susan replied, rising from her chair. "Is Gillian safely home ? I thought she might have come here for a couple of nights".

"Yes she's back safe and sound, she wanted to be in her own place, I'd be the same". Mary answered.

"Any more news about Robert's mum ?"

Susan enquired.

"She's conscious again but knocked herself about quite a bit. They're keeping her in for a few days to find the reason she fainted. Oh…you'll be pleased to know, your favourite niece is coming over to see you tomorrow".

"That's lovely, me and Gillian can have a good old girly chat. Bye the way I've been admiring that photo of Tony on your sideboard, don't you think he looks just like the fella' out of that film, South Pacific. Rossano Brazzi". Susan proclaimed.

"No, not really, don't you go letting him know that. He's conceited enough as it is without you encouraging him". Mary laughed.

+++++++++++

## Chapter Five

"What time are you expecting Gillian". Susan asked.

"I told her to come and have lunch with us, so I imagine she'll be here about twelve. How do you feel about a walk as far as Daniel's shop ?" Mary asked.

"Yes I'd love to. Do they know about us and Tony on holiday ?"

"Yes, I've told Debra, I haven't spoken to Thomas yet, and Gillian only knows we have a big surprise for her. I don't want to tell them over the phone I want show them the pictures. I did tease Gillian yesterday and got her wondering. Anyway.....Daniel's shop. Bring me something to make a nice salad". Mary said. Susan collected a plastic carrier bag from a kitchen cupboard and screwing it up tightly she left by the rear garden gate.

Susan stood in the bay window eagerly awaiting the arrival of Gillian's red Fiesta. At the first sighting she fled through the door and bounced down the path as her car came to a halt, then grabbing Gillian in a tight bear hug as she emerged from the vehicle. "Hello young lady". Susan gushed affectionately as they proceeded to walk hand in hand towards the house. Gillian let go of Susan's grip and stepped back to her car and returned carrying a black computer.

"Our wedding photos arrived while we were away, I've downloaded them all on to the laptop". Gillia announced and immediately set the machine down on the coffee table. "I did look through them last night, I think they're lovely. See what you think".

"Let's have lunch first, it's all ready. Don't you think you ought to let Robert see them before you show them to anyone else ?" Mary suggested.

"He won't mind mum". Gillian replied with a whiff of uncertainty.

Gillian sat in the centre of the settee with Mary one side and Susan the other. After many admiring comments viewing the numerous professional photographs, Mary put her hand across the keyboard to prevent Gillian from passing on to the next picture. "Who's that ?" Mary asked, pointing to a slightly out of focus female face.

"I don't know her, she's standing next to Maxine, could be a friend of hers. Her husband wasn't able to come so I did tell her to bring someone if she wanted to. Pity it looks as if she's caught a reflection from the sun. Let's pass on". Gillian uttered.

"When you've chosen your album, make an extra album for me. I'll give you the money ?" Mary stated.

"Now you've gone and ruined your Christmas present mother". Gillian joked.

"I want a couple of nice ones. I like the one of you on your own standing at your front garden gate, and the one with the both of you on the church steps and a nice group photo, which ever you decide. Have you got a price list? So that I can pay you before I go back home". Susan requested.

"I should have asked you as soon as you arrived, has Robert phoned again?" Mary muttered apologetically.

"Yes mum, he called last night. He says he's going to stay until she comes out of hospital, his uncle Ron is going to come and stay with her for a while to keep an eye on her. Anyway what about this big fantastic surprise you mentioned yesterday, I can see auntie Susan's almost bursting to say something".

An hour later Gillian was still looking bewildered and perplexed about the whole coincidence and still holding the photographs in her hands. "My God mother, you married the one, now it's about time you married the other one. You missed him the first time round. Look at him there canoodling with auntie Susan on the sea wall". Gillian chuckled and laughed at her own comments. not realising her mother's discomfort,

"Gillian ! stop talking about marriage, I get enough hints from Tony as it is. I've got one husband, he could come back one day, no one really knows if he was killed. Then what would I do ?" Mary gulped.

"Now then who wants a drink, tea or coffee ?" Susan deliberately asked to change the subject.

"Not for me, I need to get back, I haven't even unpacked yet, let alone done any washing".

+++++++++++

## Chapter Six

"Gillian was on the phone this morning while you were out walking". Mary informed.

"Is she okay ? What did she have to say ?" Susan asked.

"Robert's coming home on Sunday, he says his mother is being allowed to go home for the weekend. She's got to go back in next week for a scan and more tests. His uncle is going to look after her".

"So they don't know why she passed out then ? Let's hope it's nothing serious. Is his uncle Ron her brother ?" Susan asked.

"Yes, I think he lives quite close. He lost his wife very young, she was only in her early thirties when she died. He lives on his own, he never remarried.....Oh, for some reason Gillian said Robert's got it into his head that he was adopted".

"What's given that impression ?" Susan interrupted.

"Gillian said that while he's been staying in his mum's bungalow he's been nosing through lots of papers and old letters and documents and he found a reference saying he was born in Horsham. Apparently his mum and dad told him he was born in Saint Neots where they were living at the time. She said he's quite annoyed about it". Mary answered.

"He's probably got himself in a panic and read it all wrong". Susan said again interrupting.

"I don't think so, Gillian said he also found a letter from an adoption society dated nineteen eighty three referring to a baby boy, but there wasn't any name on it. It just thanked Mister and Missis Hines for their interest and the society would be in touch within a few days".

"It doesn't necessarily mean that he is the baby in the letter". Susan uttered.

"If it's not him the alternative could be that Robert is their son and they were considering having him adopted. You don't know what their situation was". Mary replied tongue in cheek.

"For goodness sake, keep that silly thought to yourself". Susan retorted sternly.

Mary answered the front door to be surprised by the appearance of her eldest son Thomas and his wife Elaine. "Come on in...You don't normally call on me on a Saturday unless you're off to play football".

"It is football mum, it's our first match this afternoon. Thomas replied.

"How're you Elaine, I don't get chance to see much of you since you moved out of town". Mary chirped.

"No, I know, the only real chance I

have now is to come along with Thomas. We don't have a bus service, I'd have to walk a couple of miles to the next village to the nearest stop. I keep asking him to teach me to drive, but then there's always something wrong with the car or he's busy. So he says". Elaine chuntered sarcastically.

"Anyway you're staying till Thomas gets back. Susan's here so we can have a good old natter. She's gone for a stroll along the beach. I'll show you something that'll really surprise you when she gets back".

"What's that then mum ?" Thomas asked impatiently.

Unable to contain her own excitement and wait for Susan, Mary laid the holiday photographs out on the dining table. "Take a look at that lad". Mary instructed pointing to a sixteen year old Tony.

"Who are we supposed to say it is mum ? We know the other lad is the one you married, our dad Thomas".

"It's Tony !" Mary blurted out causing her son and daughter-in-law to flop into a couple of dining chairs in disbelief. "It is him" Mary asserted. "Here's Susan now she'll tell you".

"Oh damn mum, I'm going to have to dash off. I still don't believe it. I know you and auntie Susan, couple of kidders. I'll see you when I get back". Thomas called out as he slammed the front door.

Elaine finally accepted the sister's fantastic story of the Swanage holiday and how Tony convinced them with his intimate knowledge of every detail.

"If you look closely at him in this picture you can actually recognise him". Elaine proffered.

"Gillian almost fell off her chair when we told her, I'm still wondering if she believes it. I told Debra, but Daniel wasn't in the shop".

"There you are Mary, you must have been meant for each other, it's about time, you've been together for twenty odd years, when can we expect a wedding ?" Elaine uttered mischievously with a broad grin.

"Don't you start, I have enough off our Gillian. Tony does keep asking, but I'm always afraid that my husband might one day come knocking at the door. It's not impossible.....no one really knows what did happened to him. I wouldn't know what to do if he did come back". Mary replied painfully. "Anyway, he was Susan's boyfriend". Mary added with a sorrowful smile.

The garden gate rattled on it's hinges followed by the sound of the kitchen door being roughly treated as Thomas entered on into the lounge.

"You've obviously lost by the mood you're in". Elaine stated.

"Four one, I've had it, I think it's time I packed it in, I'm too old, I can't even move, my legs are so stiff and I even had to come off the pitch with cramp. I'll keep going now for this season but I think it'll be my last".

"Gillian said Robert will be back home tomorrow so he'll be able to play next week". Mary murmured sympathetically.

"We certainly need him, he can play in place of me. Oh.....what about those Swanage photos and this ridiculous story about Tony ?" Thomas sceptically quipped.

After yet another exhausting hour of explaining and trying to convince Thomas of their extraordinary tale, Mary and Susan finally relaxed when Thomas relented and decided to accept their story.

"Come on Elaine we need to get going".

"Another ten minutes, your mum's just making us a cup of tea".


"Elaine and Thomas haven't long gone, Elaine spent the afternoon with me and Susan looking at you in Swanage". Mary informed Tony the second he entered the house.

"And what was their reaction ?" Tony

asked.

"Absolute amazement. Thomas poo poo'd it and had to dash off to his football but Elaine said she could actually recognise you. Thomas took a bit more convincing when he got back". Mary replied with several interruptions by Susan.

Susan lifted the nearest telephone receiver. "Hello auntie Susan is my mum there ?" "Just a minute Gill, Mary it's Gillian for you".

"Is everything alright Gillian ?" Mary enquired.

"I'm just ringing to let you know that Robert's home. He was intending to stay till tomorrow but his uncle Ron is staying with his mum so he told Robert to go on home. We've just got in, I picked him up from Liskeard station".

"Is his mother any better ?".

"He said she does look a lot better now they've patched her up a bit, she's still no idea what she did". Gillian replied with sigh and continued talking. "Robert's still muttering on about this adoption business. He's beginning to get on my nerves with it. Anyway mum we're off to the pub for something to eat first and then Robert wants to go through the wedding photos. I told him all about you and Susan with Tony in Swanage. He's dying to see the pictures. We're coming over to see you tomorrow, be over about two".

++++++++++++

# Chapter Seven

Mary and Susan stood chatting in the front garden with Mary's neighbour when a smiling Gillian steered her red Fiesta between the entrance pillars and gently rolled forward on to the drive. Robert and Gillian followed Mary through the rear gate and into the lounge via the French doors, leaving Susan in deep conversation with the neighbour.

"Susan's struggling to get away from Missis Parker, it was a bit naughty of us to leave her there on her own". Gillian laughed.

"It serves her right, she's the one who keeps the chat going, It's Beryl I feel sorry for. Susan's still telling all about knowing Tony fifty years ago and how he was her boyfriend on that holiday in Swanage when we were kids". Mary chuntered.

"At last you're back Susan, I've left you a cup of tea in the pot, see if it's still hot".

"That neighbour of yours is a bit of a nosy old devil, is she really named Parker? I couldn't get away. You rotten pair didn't care, leaving me there". Susan moaned.

"Yes, that is her name, but you were the one doing all the chat, she looked as though she was the one trying to escape, I was beginning to feel sorry for her". Mary said. With both sisters laughing. Susan ditched the teapot and quickly made herself a fresh mug of coffee.

"Can I see those Swanage photos now, where are they ?" Robert shouted from the lounge

"Has he thought any more about this adoption thing ?" Mary whispered to Gillian.

"What are you two whispering for, is it about me ? Usually is". Robert barked.

"I was only telling mum about your adoption, you hadn't decided what to do yet, you're still not absolutely sure about it. You're only guessing at the moment".

"I'm not". Robert squawked emphatically. "I was definitely adopted, I just don't know why mum never told me. I intend to ring uncle Ron, he must know all about it".

"If you are right". Mary started to say.

"I know I'm right". Robert interrupted sharply.

"I was going to say. If you are right, your mum probably thought it was best to leave things be after your dad left home, and then as time went on found it too difficult to tell you". Mary said sympathetically.

"Robert didn't recognise the woman on that group photo". Gillian butted in to change the subject.

"She's no one we invited. She probably is a friend of Maxine, I've never seen her before". Robert confirmed. "It's not the best picture but we've got several other groups to choose from".

Another hour passed by viewing the endless number of honeymoon photographs, including an enthusiastic in-depth and often boring description by Gillian of each picture as it appeared on the screen".

"My eyeballs are saying they need a rest". Susan chirped. "Who wants a coffee ?" She barked in order to depart in to the kitchen.

"I've had enough as well, I've already sat through them a couple of times". Robert added sarcastically.

"You rotten pair". Gillian responded in a mocked angry voice ending with a laugh as she reluctantly gave in and closed the laptop.

"How long are you staying ?" Gillian asked Susan.

"Another week, I'm going back a week tomorrow. I'd love to stay a bit longer but your uncle Walter's probably getting a bit lonely by now. Or prap's he's not !". Susan replied.

"That's alright then, we'll definitely see you again before then. We're going to get off now mum. Come on Robert".

"You can stay on and have dinner with us if you want to, you don't have to go". Mary offered.

"We would love to mum, but we've arranged to see some of Robert's friends in the pub this evening. It's one of his old college mates and his wife, they came to our evening wedding do".

"What did you reckon to the tea dance today ?" Tony asked Susan as they sat enjoying the roast beef dinner that Mary had cooked. "You're certainly no wallflower, you didn't sit out many dances".
"I loved it. It's a pity it's my last. I'll see if I can get down here again before Christmas with Walter and get him on the dance floor......I don't think !". Susan replied with a heavy sigh. "Who was the tall white haired chap, I danced with him a couple of times ? He was sitting with a group in the corner by the stage. He asked me to go dancing with him on Friday night. But he left before I had chance to see him".
"I don't blame him. That was Stanley Angwin, he's in his eighties. He realised that an evening on the dance floor with you could be fatal". Susan let out a loud laugh at Mary's comment.
Tony craftily sidled away to the comfort of his favourite armchair in the lounge while the sisters continued their chatter as they cleared the dining room and tidied up the kitchen. "I see Romeo Rossano Brazzi has

sneaked off again". Susan joked very quietly. Shall I ask him to give us his rendition of 'Some Enchanted Evening' ?"

"No you won't....don't you dare". Mary whispered while holding back the urge to laugh.

Gillian and Robert were both waiting on the pavement leaning against the garden wall. "You two sunbathing ? Have you been waiting long ?"

"No not long, only about ten minutes". Gillian replied.

"Don't step back Mary, your Thomas is here". Susan warned as his car came to a halt encroaching across the drive and two feet of pavement. "Hiya everyone". Thomas shouted as he clambered from his tired looking Jaguar, a candidate for a classic car if it was restored. "You fit, young Robert ? Let's see if we can do any better today". Robert slung his holdall into the back of the Jaguar and settled down in the front passenger seat. "We'll see you girls later". Thomas called out as he sped away.

"You girls !" Susan repeated, "Cheeky sod. I'll smack him one when he comes back". She added with a grin.

"It's far too nice to sit inside". Mary suggested. Susan and Gillian laid out the garden loungers on the sunny patio while

Mary busied herself preparing some cool refreshments. "Any more news, did Robert ring his uncle ?". Mary asked.

"Not yet, he doesn't want to put him on the spot. I think he prefers to speak to his mum first as soon as she's well enough". Gillian replied.

"Just a thought, I really hadn't ought to suggest this, but do you think it could be possible that Robert is their son and they were considering having him adopted. You don't know what their situation was at the time. Whatever you do don't repeat this to Robert". Mary said, with immediate regret.

"I'd never thought of that...surely not". Gillin said, now shocked into a temporary silence.

"What does Robert intend to do now ?" Mary enquired attempting to distract from her comment.

"He's already made a start, he went on the internet to the West Sussex registry office last night and ordered a birth certificate".

"But his surname wouldn't have been Hines, I don't see how that'll work". Mary wondered.

"He's just taking a chance that they might look for an alternate name. He stated that he was born in Horsham hospital and put his date of birth and he hopes Robert Stewart were his original names. He said that Hines is his adopted name".

"That all sounds possible, let's hope he hears back pretty soon". Mary uttered.

"I hope so, he's driving me up the wall". He talks about nothing else".

"Whatever you do, for goodness sake don't mention what I said earlier. I should never had even suggested it". Mary pleaded attempting to extricate herself.

"You're keeping quiet auntie Susan, you've not said a lot".

"I hope it all works out well for him. And I told you....Mary....to keep that idea to yourself". Susan snapped chastising her younger sister.

"Are you looking forward to going back home ?" Gillian asked, to defuse the current topic of conversation.

"No, I can't say I am. I think your uncle Walter wants me back, if only to cook his meals. Only joking ! I've had a lovely holiday. You're very lucky to live in such a beautiful place. You've got your mum and dad to thank for that for moving down here".

"Have you never thought about moving to the coast". Susan asked.

"Oh I've dreamed about it very often, but that's about as far as it gets. The sale of our house wouldn't buy us a beach hut here. And I'd never manage to prize that husband of mine from the true love of his life". Susan replied disdainfully.

"What's his true love ?" Gillian quipped and grinned as she waited for Susan's funny remark.

"Bloomin' Aston Villa, he'd stand on the terraces all day watching the grass grow if they'd let him". Susan replied annoyingly.

"That sounds like the boys are back". Susan commented referring to the noisy banter coming from the other side of the front door.

"Well,,,..how did you get on then ?" Gillian asked sarcastically, holding the door open as they carried on into the lounge.

"Two...Two. And he scored them both". Thomas announced.

"Who scored the other two ?" Gillian asked keeping a straight face.

"Very funny". Robert quipped, ignoring his wife's joke, not appearing in the mood for Gillian's sense of humour.

"Have you had any results of your mum's tests ?" Mary asked.

"Yes, uncle Ron left me a text while we were playing. He spoke to the hospital this morning and they told him that mum has a brain tumour".

"Oh God, I am sorry". Mary murmured followed by similar responses from Gillian and Susan.

"My uncle Ron was told that it isn't malignant, the lady doctor who rang him told him to bring her back into hospital for eight o'clock on Monday for an operation to have it removed". Robert carefully explained.

"I'm sure she'll be fine". Mary uttered sincerely. "You'll get some good news by Monday night". She added positively.

"Are you ready Gill ?" Robert asked.

"We're going to love you and leave you now auntie Susan, hope we see you before Christmas. Have a good journey and give my love to uncle Walter and to gran next time you visit her". Gillian said.

"Tom". Robert called out. "Are you staying on ? Your Jag's across the drive".

"No, I'm off now anyway, I won't be a minute". Thomas answered. "Bye then mum". Thomas then gave his glamorous aunt a loving hug. "See you soon Susie". He quipped.

"I'll give you Susie". Susan chirped with a loud laugh. "But I did appreciate that hug". She added.

Mary and Susan stood on the pavement, waving as first Thomas's and then Gillian's car went from view.

"Three gone, now another one's turned up, I just heard his car. I'll get the door". Susan cried out enthusiastically.

"For goodness sake Susan, sit back down, he'll let himself in, he's got his own key". Mary squeaked.

"Evening lovely ladies, something smells delicious. It must be you two girls". Tony gushed..

"Sis...Is this handsome bloke of yours complimenting us or insulting your cooking".

"You can take it as a compliment but he can forget about any dinner tonight". Mary responded, laughing as Tony wrapped both his arms around her waste and gave her a loving kiss.

"Oh my God, it's time you married this lovely man before I decide to divorce Walter". Susan chirped.

"Right ladies, now I've finished milking your admiration here's the copies of the Swanage pictures, there's three sets there". Tony advised placing the prints and the original photographs on the coffee table.

After the evening meal Susan chose to relax in an armchair clutching her set of prints in one hand and a copy of the Peoples Friend laid open on her lap as tiredness overcame her. Her eyes grew heavy and slowly closed, the photographs slipped from her hand on to the open magazine. Tony looked across at Mary and nodded in the direction of Susan and smiled as he hopped around the television channels.

Mary wandered to her desk in the hall and returned with her stuffed full scrap book. Putting her feet up and stretching full length on to the settee, and after refixing the original pictures back into the album, proceeded to eagerly record Tony's account and his memories from fifty years ago of their Swanage holiday.

In the far corner of the lounge, the television was showing a gardening program. Tony had nodded off in his favourite chair with Susan fast asleep in the other. "Thanks for the company you two". Mary chuntered as she tip toed between the coffee table and the armchairs to retrieve the remote control from Tony's loose grip and then return to slouch full length back onto the settee.

Mary gave Susan a gentle tap on her shoulder. "Wake up.....it's bed time". Susan opened her eyes with a dazed expression.

"Where's Tony ?"

"He went home half an hour ago, it's well past midnight, I've made a hot drink, so drink up and let's get to bed". Mary urged.

"Will I see Tony again before I leave ?" Susan asked desperately.

"He'll be here tomorrow evening and I daresay we'll have our usual stroll to the pub".

The sisters laughed hysterically at each other's clumsy attempt to negotiate the two feet drop from the promenade onto the sandy beach. "It's a good job no one's down this end of the beach to witness that brilliant performance". Mary said as they continued laughing.

After a short visit to the town centre. A smallish holiday resort with it's main shopping area set back from the sea front nestling behind a row of brightly painted terraced guest houses. Beyond lays an almost empty rundown amusement arcade bellowing out pop music. Mary and Susan returned to walk the short distance along the promenade and entered into Daniel and Debra's corner stores.

"Oh hello you two". Debra shouted as Susan held the shop door open for the last customer to depart. "Daniel" She shouted again but much louder in order to extract him from the stock room.

"Mary told us all about your incredible Swanage story. Fancy not knowing you'd met him fifty years ago, and that he was your date and Mary married the other lad. It all sounds unbelievable !". Debra gushed excitedly. "You'll be able to dine out on this story for ever". Debra added with a smile.

"We've just popped in for me to say goodbye, I'm off home tomorrow". Susan said sorrowfully". Marry disappeared to the rear of the store to collect her Sunday paper, and after paying for her purchase, along with Debra, joined Susan and Daniel outside the shop in the sunshine. Daniel and Debra both in turn gave Susan an affectionate embrace. The sisters crossed the shore road and staying on the sea side of the promenade continued their stroll back to Mary's house.

"That's enough walking for me for today". Mary proclaimed on reaching her home. Tony and Susan lagged a few yards behind deep in conversation. "You two do realise that walk to the pub and back was four miles ? on top of the couple of miles we walked this morning. I'm exhausted". She added as she observed Susan and Tony affectionately holding hands. "Are you coming in for a while ?" Mary interrupted.

"No, I think I'll head off, it's quite late. I've said my goodbye to Susan". Tony replied, but before climbing into his Mercedes he gave Susan another emotional hug and a kiss on both cheeks. "Have a safe journey and I'll see you again soon. I still can't believe we kissed and cuddled fifty years ago".

Susan looked very upset as Mary left her standing alone on the pavement. Tears began to trickle down her cheeks as she continued waving and watching as Tony drove towards the sea front and out of sight.

Mary looked on as Susan climbed on the bus and sat in the front window seat. The bus driver lifted the several items of luggage into the hold as the remaining passengers filed aboard. The automatic doors closed. Mary waited until the bus departed the station before returning to her car to begin the journey home.

The solitude of the drive home from Plymouth allowed Mary to revisit the events of the past two weeks, and her thoughts returned to the black and white Swanage holiday snapshots.

She began to imagine the outcome if Susan had dated Thomas and she Tony during that brief three day romance fifty years ago. Would Thomas still have come knocking their door for her sister and would she have ever kept in touch with Tony?

Although she idolised and adored her elder sister she couldn't prevent a slight guilty feeling of envy at the attention she'd received during her stay, in particular the reference to the discovery that she was Tony's date on holiday and the affection that Tony had displayed towards her.

Mary's focus was immediately brought

back to the present through a lapse of concentration when she narrowly managed to avoid an accident. The slow moving queue of traffic suddenly came to a halt with Mary's mind wandering, causing her to brake hard and stop within a few inches of a large lorry.

Mary was relieved to safely reach home and delighted to find Tony waiting in the open doorway.

++++++++++++

## Chapter Eight

"Susan certainly made an impression at the dances, they all wanted to know when she would be coming again, especially the fellas". Tony remarked.

"Especially you ! If she'd stayed much longer I would have begun to get worried". Mary replied with a nervous laugh.

"Oh....come on....you weren't seriously thinking that. You should know me well enough by now. I want to marry you...you daft devil". Tony chuntered

"No, course not, and I want to marry you one day. And I know how unfair it's been on you having to keep our secret all these years". Mary sighed as the ringing of the telephone curtailed the conversation.

"It's only me mum". Gillian announced and then informed Mary that Robert's mother is having her operation. "Robert's uncle is going to ring the minute he knows anything". Gillian paused for a few moments shuffling one handed to unfold a letter. "Robert had a reply to his birth certificate application this morning. It says they cannot assist him in this matter and that he needs to obtain his adoption file. And it says he can do this on line on the Government web site. He had a quick look but gave up".

"I heard, I was on the line in the hall".

Tony stated as Mary was about to relay Gillian's call. "He's not going to get his original birth certificate, he might as well ask his uncle outright. He obviously knows all the details".

The following morning Mary made her monthly visit to the nearest supermarket situated about three miles away on an area resembling an industrial estate, with several other large popular stores also occupying the site. Leaving the stores, Mary pushed her wayward out of control shopping trolley at an awkward angle in an attempt to steer a straight path across the busy car park back to her Mercedes. With her shopping loaded into the boot and the trolley located in it's designated shelter ready for the next unfortunate unsuspecting shopper, Mary let out a sigh of relief as she drove away from the car park.

The mobile telephone hiding in Mary's handbag resting on the passenger seat rang for several seconds before ringing again for a further short period. Mary eventually found a convenient flat section of roadside verge to draw to a halt.

"Hello mum. I guess you're driving. I'll ring you again tonight, something exciting to tell you". Gillian's voice mail announce.

Mary's curiosity was too much and

made her reply immediately hoping to talk to her daughter, but this time the call went on to Gillian's voice mail. Having realised that her daughter would now be back in class she re-joined the traffic to complete her journey home.

Still impatient to hear Gillian's news, Mary made several attempts throughout the afternoon to make contact without success, reluctantly giving in and deciding to wait to be contacted

"Hello…Gillian, .I've been trying to call you. I got your message". Mary squawked eagerly as the telephone finally rang.

"Yes I know, I was on my lunch break at the time. Anyway…first bit of good news, Robert's mum came through the operation without any problems and she is going to be alright". Mary could sense that Gillian was bursting at the seams with excitement about something. "He did ask his uncle about the adoption and he told Robert it was true, but he was reluctant to say a lot, he preferred that Robert talked to his mother about it when she's better". Mary held the receiver to her ear as she listened to what she thought sounded like the rustling of paper. "This is the really astonishing thing". Gillian began again bubbling with emotion. "Robert had this letter this morning….He's got a sister !!".

"What on earth are you babbling on about Gillian".

"It's true ! He has got a sister". Gillian repeated emphatically. "He has, he got this letter this morning".

"What letter ?" Mary snapped.

"It's from a company called Worldwide Search Limited".

Mary barged in. "What does Robert think about it ?"

"He doesn't know yet, he'd left this morning before the post came, and I can't contact him because he's in school and he won't be switched on".

"Don't you think you should have let him open his own letter ?" Mary added.

"For goodness sake mum, do you want to know about his sister or not, Stop interrupting me !" Gillian paused for a few seconds assuming her mother was about to retaliate. "Anyway, I'll start again.....It's from a company called Worldwide Search. They say that over the past year they have been carrying out a search on behalf of Jane Barnes and obtained conclusive information that Robert Stewart Hines is her brother. It says she wishes to meet Robert. The letter goes on to say they will understand if he declines or needs time to decide. It then gives a name of John Ryalls as a contact".

"This all seems just too much of a coincidence. He's just found out that he was adopted, now this. Think about it Gillian, it all seems a bit suspicious to me". Mary replied seriously.

"Why would anyone want to pretend they was his sister. He's not famous and he's certainly not worth anything. We don't have two pennies to rub together, so she can't be after his money. Anyway, I think she's genuine". Gillian snapped sharply.

"Well if she is, he's now got something he didn't have before, he's got a new surname". Mary quipped.

"I'll try and get hold of Robert as soon as school's over and I'll let you know what he thinks. We'll be round on Saturday lunch time for football. Robert will bring the letter, you can read it for yourself. Bye mum". Mary popped the handset onto it's base and dropped exhausted on to the settee.

The sound of the front door opening brought Mary back on her feet. "Are you in here ?" Tony shouted, pushing open the lounge door.

"You'll never guess what Gillian told me an hour ago". Mary muttered. "She said Robert has received a letter from some genealogists telling him that he has a sister somewhere, and she wants to meet him".

"You are joking ?" Tony retorted.

"No, Gillian got very excited about it, and got very annoyed with me for not taking it seriously".

"What's Robert said about it ?" Tony asked.

"He hadn't seen it then, he probably has by now, I'm waiting for her to ring me".

"It sounds a bit strange to me, with Robert talking about the possibility of him being adopted. It all seems too much of a coincidence". Tony replied cynically. "Anyway is there any news about his mum ?".He added.

"Robert says she's going to be fine".

"With all this excitement I haven't got round to starting anything for dinner. Do you fancy the chip shop ?" Mary asked.

"Yes that's okay, I'll nip out now if you're ready to eat. Share a large fish ?"

Mary anxiously grabbed the telephone before it had chance to ring a second time.

"Mum". Gillian chipped

"Has he read it, what does he think ?" Mary blurted out.

"He hasn't put it down yet. He keeps reading it over and over. He's worried about it. He wants it to be true, but he's a bit sceptical about it".

"Is he going to reply to it ? Does he

want to meet her ?" Mary enquired.

"Oh he really wants meet her if it's true. Before he rings this John Ryalls he's going to have another go at getting his birth certificate. He's going to use Barnes as his surname and he's not going to mention anything about adoption". Gillian gushed.

"That should be interesting, he's not going to bother with his adoption file then ?" Mary asked.

"Not yet, now he's got this name, if nothing comes of it I daresay he will then".

"You heard all that, what did you think ?" Mary asked Tony as he returned to the kitchen.

"If he does manage to get a correct birth certificate using that name it would seem that this girl is genuine....let's hope he's not in for another upset".

"Pop the fish and chips in to the microwave for a minute". Mary instructed while she quickly laid the table. After a couple of "pings" they finally sat to enjoy their evening meal.

+++++++++++

# Chapter Nine

"That'll be them now". Mary uttered.

Robert marched through the hallway grinning like a Cheshire cat with Gillian hot on his heels anxiously trying to be the first to tell the news.

"Robert's got his birth certificate, it came this morning". She blurted out.

"Go on then, what does it say ?" Mary asked urgently. Gillian jumped in and again beat Robert to be the bearer of the news.

"Everything checks out, it's his original birth certificate. His full name and his date of birth and the place he was born, it's all there. It's fantastic mum".

"I'll have to see it later, come on Robert we'll have to go, we're meant to be at the ground for half one, it's about an hours bus ride today". Thomas said ushering his brother-in-law from the house.

"It's good news all round. His mum came through the operation well and they reckon she'll be on a general ward in a few days time and they expect to send her home about a week later". Gillian advised.

"Is Robert going to see her ?" Mary asked.

"He's already had a word with his headmaster about having the time away and he's going to go this Tuesday and staying on till Friday". Gillian said at the same time fumbling with excitement trying to retrieve the copy of Robert's birth certificate from it's envelope then handing it to her mother. Mary unfolded the A4 sheet of paper and casting her eyes from left to right, silently read the type written columns.

When and where born... *Tenth of January 1983 Flat 7 Eldridge Ct. Horsham.*
Name if Any....*Robert Stewart*
Sex.....*Boy*
Name and Surname of Father.....*Thomas Barnes*
Name and Maiden Surname of Mother..... *Katherine Jane Stewart*
Rank or Profession of Father.....*Not known*
Signature, Description and Residence of Informant......*K.J.Stewart Mpther Flat 7 Eldridge Court Jules Eldridge Close Horsham*
When Registered......*Thirty first of January 1983* Signature of Registrar....*Herbert Lockhart*

Gillian passed the letter Robert had received from the genealogists to Mary. After memorising the information on the birth certificate she carefully read the letter a couple of times before returning both the items back to her daughter. "Well it looks like he's got himself a new sister". Mary gasped. "What does he intend to do now ?" She asked.

"Well now he's convinced that she's real. He's going to contact this Worldwide company on Monday. He's started to wonder why there was no mention about their parents or if there's any more relations he doesn't know about". Gillian replied.

"Has he had a word with his uncle ?" Mary asked.

"He phoned him just before we came out. His uncle said he didn't know anything about it and was surprised. What time are you expecting Tony mum ?"

"Oh, not until seven".

"We might be gone by then, but you'll have plenty to talk about. I was going to offer to leave the letter and the certificate for him to see, but I think Robert might need them when he speaks to this fella Ryalls". Gillian replied.

"That's all right, he can see them another time, I'll tell him all he needs to know".

The jovial banter coming from the front porch got Gillian up from the comfort of her chair. "Tony's here as well mum". Gillian shouted on opening the door. "I thought you'd be back sooner, It sounds as you might have even won a match". She added.

"Three nil...three . nil". Robert repeated exuberantly, while still bubbling over with the excitement of meeting his sister. "Show Tony". He urged.

"Show me what ?.......Oh my God, you got it then". Tony chirped and quickly read the document. "Well you proved me wrong, I never believed it was true. How does it feel to know you've got a new sister ?" He added loudly.

"Let's hope he finds a new sister every Saturday morning, it certainly improved his football. Let's have a butcher's". Thomas joked. "Anyway I'm off now.....Oi ! Robert, best of luck on Monday with your phone call, and I hope your mum gets well soon. Let me know about the match next Saturday just in case you decide to stay on".

Gillian finally managed to interrupted Tony and Robert's deep conversation.

"It's time we went as well, mum needs to get a meal". Gillian grunted and gave her husband a sharp tug on his jacket sleeve.

"You know I was telling you about the unknown woman on the wedding photo. Well Gillian thought it could be his sister. You know, it could be". Mary suggested.

"If it was her why did she disappear, and how did she find out that Robert was getting married or where to find him. The agency could never afford to give her that information. They could be in a lot of trouble if they did before any agreement had been reached". Tony advocated in his infinite wisdom.

++++++++++++

# Chapter Ten

Mary stood in the lounge watching intently at the rivers of rainwater racing each other down the windows as she waited patiently for Tony to arrive to collect her for the afternoon tea dance. Prompt as ever at two o'clock, his pale blue Mercedes pulled up across the drive.

Always the perfect gentleman with umbrella already open for Mary to step under as she opened her front door. Then displaying his less gentlemanly side with his greeting. "Bloody weather !"

"Gillian rang me this morning before she went off to school, she'd just taken Robert to Liskeard station. She said he rang the fellow at the genealogist company yesterday afternoon as soon as he got home. They are now going to let her know that Robert does want to meet her, but she's not in this country, she lives in Italy, she lives in Rome". Mary told Tony as he drove along the seafront.

"That's a bit inconvenient, who's going to visit who ? Where would they meet ? Let's hope she's wealthy". Tony joked

With the tea dance over for another week, Mary and Tony finally managed to weave their way past the noisy chattering group of guests congregated in the hotel reception lobby and escape out into the damp air. The ground was still very wet from the earlier rain fall and the couple skipped around the car park avoiding the isolated surface puddles and crossed to the extreme furthest corner and to where Tony had parked his Mercedes.

Tony drove away from the hotel car park and proceeded to drive in the opposite direction to normal. "Where are we going ?" Mary queried.

"I thought we'd go over to my place for dinner tonight for a change. I'm going to do the cooking". Tony answered with a smile.

"This is a first, this should be good. What are we having ?" Mary asked.

"Wait and see, it's all prepared, I did it this morning". Tony replied proudly.

After a twenty minute drive through a series of country lanes the Mercedes turned through a gap between a row of tall birch trees and entered a two hundred yard long private asphalt single lane driveway leading to an imposing Edwardian property. The private drive being isolated on either side by a rustic timber ranch style fence enclosing a pasture with sheep lazily grazing on the right and with half a dozen horses roaming the field opposite.

Mary kicked off her shoes at the lounge door before stepping on to the lush pile carpet and slumping down into a comfortable plain mustard coloured fabric armchair while Tony immediately disappeared into the kitchen. "It's all cooking !" He shouted through the partially open door. "Be about an hour". He added as he joined Mary in the lounge.

Mary's curiosity was aroused and she couldn't resist the temptation to pop in the kitchen to see what was in the oven.

"It's no point poking your nose, it's covered with foil, you can't see what it is". Tony joked. "And it's no good looking in the fridge either".

"Oh.....come on.....what is it ?" Mary pleaded.

"I'm not going to tell you, it's the chef's special. Just wait".

Mary sneaked a peak through the open kitchen door to see Tony dropping a 'boil in the bag' of rice in to a pan of boiling water. "Right then". Tony shouted causing Mary to quickly dodge back in to the lounge. "Go and sit at the table in the dining room, It's all laid up". A few minutes later Tony entered carrying a rectangular glass oven dish, minus it's tin foil cover and placed it down on a table mat. "It's with rice, I hope you'll like it".

After consuming a plate of food larger than normal, Mary gasped. "I'm impressed, that was a beautiful meal".

"Good, I'm glad you enjoyed it, we'll have our pudding in the lounge with a coffee". Tony responded.

"Pudding as well". Mary chirped. "You know something, I can just see your nearest neighbour's farm buildings. Haven't you ever thought about selling this big old house and moving somewhere less isolated ?"

"That's exactly what I am about to suggest. Let's get married and buy a house together". Tony proposed hopefully.

"I knew this is what the meal was all about, It's a lovely idea, but not yet". Mary retorted emphatically and rose from the table and returned to the lounge. "Hurry up with the pudding". She laughed, dispelling Tony's hopes of a Christmas wedding. "I wonder.....what if it had been me and you together fifty years ago in Swanage, would you have come knocking on my door like Thomas did ?"

"Yes of course I would". Tony replied instantly.

"I doubt it". Mary chuntered and then began an evening of nostalgic memories surrounding those few days together, and their past twenty five years since.

"There's one thing for sure, you won't

have the neighbours gossiping about me staying over at your place". Mary chirped as the Mercedes sped along the private driveway towards the country lane passing the inquisitive herd of sheep all grazing within a few feet of the fence. The horses also seemed to be interested, their heads reaching beyond the fence rails to gnaw at the long grassy tufts.

"You're looking at my neighbours, all they're interested in is chewing grass". Tony laughed.

"You can drop me at the amusement arcade, I want to pop into the High Street".

"I'll park up and wait". Tony offered.

"No, you go on, I'll be a while, I'll see you this evening". Mary closed the passenger door and waited on the footpath as Tony reversed the car to make his return journey. Mary felt pleased that Tony didn't persist as she was looking forward to a stroll along the promenade and a chance to call on Daniel and Debra.

+++++++++++

# Chapter Eleven

"It's only me". Tony cried out as he opened the front door.

"It had better be". Mary shouted. "You're the only one with a key"

"Do you know if Robert's home yet ?".

"Gillian's on her way to Liskeard to meet him now, his train gets in just after seven, she rang me an hour ago. She said Robert's got a reply from his sister, well she assumes it is, it's post marked Roma". Mary informed.

"And she's hasn't opened it ?" Tony quipped.

"Doesn't seem like it, she must have taken some notice of us. Especially when she thinks there's a photo inside". Mary replied. "She sounded almost hysterical with excitement".

"Has she told Robert, I bet her little fingers are itching to open it". Tony chirped.

"No, she's not said anything to him. She said she wants to surprise him".

"She'll do that alright !" Tony replied.

"They'll be over tomorrow for football, Gillian said she'd bring the letter. I'm expecting her to give me a call as soon as Robert's opened it".

Mary said goodnight to Tony, and as

she watched from the porch the security lighting faded into darkness, and the red rear glow of Mercedes disappeared from view. Mary closed the door and immediately lifted the telephone from the hall desk before it had chance to ring for a second time. "Gillian are you alright". Mary gasped.

"Yes mum, I'm fine, sorry it's so late, we've only just got in but I thought you'd want to know. Robert's mum was moved on to a general ward today and he stayed until she was settled, that's why we're late".

"And is she alright". Mary asked.

"Yes, everything's going well, she should be home in a few days".

"And what about Robert's letter ?" Mary uttered.

"Don't ask me how I did it, but I waited till we sat in the car and put the interior light on, and then I handed it to him. His hands trembled trying to open the envelope and he burst into tears when he saw her picture. Mum.....she's absolutely beautiful, very stylish, proper Italian look".

"And what did she say in the letter ?" Mary again asked impatiently.

"She says she can come to England at a moments notice, she's married. She never mentioned any other brothers or sisters or if she has any children. I'll bring it tomorrow you can read it for yourself".

"How's Robert now ? I bet he's a bit excited".

"A bit, more than a bit, he hasn't put her photo down yet. He's just gone to bed and took it with him. I can't see either of us getting any sleep tonight". Gillian said.

The clock on the sideboard displayed twenty five past one as Mary stood staring out of her lounge window looking towards the sea front anxiously waiting to catch sight of Gillian's red Fiesta. "They'll be here soon mum, Robert would never be late for a match". Thomas advised. A further ten minutes past by before Mary scurried to open the front door the moment Gillian's car crunched to a halt on the drive.

"It's all his fault we're late mum, he wouldn't get off the laptop. He's been trying to find her house on Google Earth".

"You on about me again ?" Robert called from the pavement while tossing his gear on to the rear seat of Thomas's Jaguar. "There's no point me coming in, we'll have to dash. You ready Tom ?" Robert shouted out as Thomas emerged in the doorway.

"Elaine's on her way here, Thomas dropped her in town". Mary explained. "Well, come on, show me the letter and the photo" Mary urged. "Oh my God, she's gorgeous".

She gasped and carefully unfolded the letter and began to read.


*2 Oct. 2007*

*Villa Sogno*
*Via del Tibolsci*
*San Lorenzo*
*Roma*

*Dearest Robert*
*I'm so pleased and excited to have found you and can't wait to meet you. I was so pleased to hear that you want to meet me. I always knew I had a brother, I was seven when you where born. Our mother sadly died in hospital a few weeks later.*
*I don't know if you ever tried to find our parents. I was born in Rhodesia. Our father sent us to England just before Christmas in 1982. I remember mum telling me it was for our safety. We never saw him again. I've tried for years to find out what happened to him.*
*You were born in the flat where me and mum where living when we came to England. After mum died*

*you were taken away and I never saw you again. I was put into care and then in to several foster homes.*

*I do hope you've had a good life. Hope you have lovely kind parents. I can't wait for your reply. Please choose where you would like to meet. I am ready to fly to England at a moments notice.*

*I am married to a lovely Italian man named Gianni Russo, we've been married thirteen years now.*

*I enclose a recent photo.*

*With love, looking forward to seeing you bro'*

*Jane xxxxxx*

Having thoroughly read the letter twice, and with a trace of tears trickling down her face, Mary handed the letter back to Gillian while still holding on to the photograph.

"This is Robert's sister". Mary gushed before Elaine had stepped beyond the threshold and then ushered her into the lounge.

"Wow….she's nice, she's lovely. I'm glad they're sisters or I'd have to keep an eye on Thomas". Elaine replied.

"She's married….to an Italian, so I don't think you need worry. Show Elaine the letter Gillian". Mary chirped excitedly.

After a few minutes, and also with damp cheeks, Elaine passed the letter and the photograph back to Gillian's outstretched hands.

"Has Robert any idea when he will meet her ?" Elaine asked, wiping her eyes with a tissue.

"He's drafted out a rough reply, but he can't see his head letting him have any more school term time off. He could make it a weekend but he wants more time with her, so I think he's going to wait till half term now, it's only two weeks away". Gillian replied. "He is going to be cheeky and have a word with the head before he posts his letter to her". Gillian glanced across at her mother. "Oh mother, you'll have me crying again in a minute". She quipped.

"While you two are sorting yourselves out I'll put the kettle on for a cup of tea". Elaine joked.

For the next couple of hours, mum, daughter and daughter-in-law past away the time discussing and deciding when and where they should meet and what Robert should say and do.

"Oh my God.....just listen to us lot going on with our advise. As if Robert's going to take a blind bit of notice of anything we suggest". Gillian uttered to end the conversation.

"That sounds like our men". Elaine pulled open the front door with Tony hanging on to his key still inserted in the lock, then feigning a stumble in to the hall. "It's not the boys, it's old whatshisname". She shouted laughing at Tony's antics.

"Who's this whatshisname ?, and a bit less of the old". Tony jokingly retaliated and then with his arm around Elaine the two of them squeezed through the lounge door side by side roaring with laughter.

"He gets dafter every time I see him". Elaine said cheekily.

"Well stop encouraging the silly old fool, he still thinks he's a ladies man....he wishes !" Mary chipped in.

"What's the big secret ? what are you all grinning at ?" Tony enquired seeing the wide eyed expression on Gillian's face. "Has Robert heard from his sister ?"

Gillian nodded and handed Tony the letter.

"This must be the lads now". Mary remarked upon hearing the door bell ring.

Elaine again acting as doorman answered the call. Robert and Thomas followed her through to the lounge. "Another three points. Four two". Robert bragged.

"They've not let you win again". Gillian replied sarcastically.

Tony quietly read the letter and then exchanged it with Gillian for the photograph.

"Wow, she is nice !" Tony exclaimed, and pretended to secrete it into his jacket pocket with Thomas hovering for a glimpse of the picture.

"Wow, yes she's very nice". Thomas gushed, concurring with Tony.

"Well it's unanimous then, that's what Elaine said". Mary chuntered. "Now put your eyeballs back in their sockets".

"Get a move on Robert, we're all dying to meet her". Thomas quipped. "We're going to pop off now, we're going to call in on Dan and Debs. Is it okay to tell them Robert ?"

"Course you can, Gillian was going to give them a ring this evening anyway. Tell them we'll be over to see them tomorrow about lunchtime with the photo. We'd come with you now but we're meeting friends tonight for a drink". Robert answered.

Mary joined the queue in the hallway following behind Thomas, Elaine, Robert and Gillian out to the kerbside and leaned on the Jaguar open window to whisper to Thomas. "What did your mum say ?" Elaine asked while pulling at her seat belt.

"She thinks Debra might have something to tell us".

"She told me this morning, but she asked me not to say anything, so act surprised". Mary muttered.

"You're as bad as Gillian, no one should ever trust either of you with a secret". Thomas said and quietly laughed.

"Cheeky devil". Mary retorted with a smile as Thomas slowly drove away leaving the drive access clear for Gillian to reverse on to the road.

Mary resisted the temptation to reveal her news again and watched and waved as the red Fiesta went from sight.

Back indoors with only Tony to hear, Mary felt secure to tell her secret. "Tony... I called in the shop this morning and Debra told me that they are going to have a baby. I couldn't say anything, she wanted to tell people herself, and she'd sworn me to secrecy".

"That was a bit silly of Debra, you and secrets don't go well together. Still it's about time you became a grandmother. When is it due ?" Tony responded.

"A while yet, she's only just had it

confirmed. There's one secret I have kept". Mary replied without elaborating.

+++++++++++

# Chapter Twelve

"I'm very surprised you haven't gone with Robert to Gatwick". Mary exclaimed as Gillian swung her legs out of her car scuffing the shingle drive surface.

"No, I would have gone had Jane's Italian husband been coming, but Robert decided to go on his own as she was alone. I would have loved to be there but I think it's going to be a very emotional meeting".

"Do you know how long she intends to stay ?, obviously she's going to stay with you". Mary asked.

"She hasn't said, but I hope she stays at least while we're on half term. I hope she stays longer, we'll see". Gillian replied. "He's probably beginning to panic a bit by now, her plane lands in half an hour. Oh God was he nervous this morning, we hardly slept last night, neither of us could stop talking about her, and he insisted on leaving early and we had to wait for almost an hour at Liskeard for his train". Gillian added with a sigh of relief..

"I assume he did get to Gatwick". Mary quipped.

"Yes....he gave me a call the minute he arrived, so, so-far so good".

"Have you heard how his mum's

coping now she's back home ?" Mary asked.

"According to his uncle Ron she seems back to her old self except she still can't remember falling. She was very upset when his uncle told her that Robert knew about being adopted and she'd never told him. And she got emotional when she heard he'd found out that he had a sister". Gillian replied.

"Does she know today is the big day ?"

"Robert rang and told her a week ago, as soon as he knew his uncle had told her about the adoption. He said there was a lot of crying down the phone, but he told her everything was fine and that he understood why she hadn't told him. She said she had no idea that his birth mother had died or that he had a sister. At the end of the call both of them were crying". Gillian answered.

"Thomas won't be bothering to call here this lunchtime with Robert not playing today, he'll just go straight to the ground, so let's go for a stroll along the beach into town and have lunch, by the time we get back we should hear from Robert". Mary suggested.

"That sounds a good idea, I'll just grab my coat from the car".

"You've only just missed Gillian". Mary

informed Tony the moment he stepped in to the hallway.

"Have you heard anything yet, has Robert phoned?" Tony asked hopefully.

"No, not yet, we were hoping to get a call when we came back from town, but I suppose they've got a lot of catching up to do. At least they must have met by now or Robert would have rung. He's bound to ring once they're on the train to let Gillian know a time to meet them".

"Thank you for dinner Mary, delicious as usual. I'll clear up, you go and put your feet up". Tony offered taking Mary by surprise.

"You don't have to keep complimenting the food, you have dinner here every day. You can wash up if you want, I'll call the doctor when you've finished to find out what's wrong with you". Mary joked and wandered into the lounge and dropped full length on to the settee. "And I'll have a biscuit with my coffee when you're ready". She shouted.

"You're not going to be meeting Jane this evening now". Tony uttered as he entered the lounge and placed a couple of hot mugs onto the coffee table.

"I know that, I was never expecting them tonight, Gillian will give me a call as soon as she knows something". Mary retorted slightly harshly

Tony twisted his favourite armchair to square up to the television and promptly pressed his head against the backrest. Mary watched as during the next ten minutes or so he struggled to prevent his eyes from closing, finally falling sound asleep. "Oh well, on my own again". Mary murmured to herself.

The late October Sunday morning was quite chilly with a strong onshore breeze reddening Mary's face as she walked back home after collecting her morning newspaper from Daniel and Debra's stores. Immediately she entered the front door she was alerted by the flashing light on the answer machine. "You have one new message". The machine responded when Mary pressed the button. "Hello mum, Jane's here, we'll be round this evening to introduce her, about seven, ring me if that's a problem". Gillian's excited voice echoed. "End of message". Concluded the faceless voice. "No, that's no trouble at all". A delighted Mary told herself.

Still wearing her winter coat Mary quickly collected the keys to her Mercedes, dashed from the house and with one exhaustive heave raised the garage door. Swiftly reversing the car the full length of the drive out on to the street and speeding the short distance to the sea front and within minutes drawing to a rapid halt back at the corner shop.

"Have you forgotten something Mary ?" Debra laughed as Mary almost took the door off it's hinges in her haste.

"Gillian left me a message. They're coming round tonight with Robert's sister to meet me. I need something a bit special". Mary gulped breathlessly.

"Yes Gillian has just this second rung me to tell me Jane had arrived. She did suggest we come to your house tonight, but I thought it would be a bit overpowering for her to have the whole family there gawping at her, so we're meeting Thomas and Elaine and going to Gillian's tomorrow night". Debra uttered.

"I've already got a good bottle of champagne we didn't open last Christmas but I could do with a couple of bottles of decent wine". Mary chirped.

"Try these ones, these are our most expensive wines". Debra announced as she placed the two bottles into a wire basket. One red and one white. "Now you'll find we have some nice goodies in the chiller". She added.

Debra lifted Mary's two laden baskets on to the counter and carefully packed the contents in to plastic bags, brushing aside Mary's hand as she attempted to pay for the goods. "Have these on the house, you've spent enough in this shop over the years". Debra retorted.

Mary gratefully thanked Debra and with a bag in each hand returned to her car and the short journey home, driving the Mercedes directly into the already open garage.

Tony duly arrived on time, two hours earlier than usual as Mary had requested. "You startled me". Mary squealed as Tony quietly sneaked unnoticed into the kitchen and wrapped his arms around her waist.

"Come in like yourself next time, you frightened the life out of me". Mary gulped as she composed herself and continued preparing ever more sandwiches.

"Where are the cakes I asked you to get ?" Mary snapped, fully expecting Tony to have forgotten them. Without further question Tony left the room and returned bearing a neatly packed box of assorted cream cakes, floating the box under Mary's nose as he placed it in the fridge. "I'd left them on the back seat". He retaliated playfully.

"That's everything all ready". Mary stated staring admiringly at the array of well presented food. "Right, now I'm going to get changed".

"What for, you look pretty fantastic as you are. it's Robert's sister we're meeting, not the Queen". Tony quipped.

"Flatterer, and a liar. I see you're wearing your best suit". Mary shouted from half way up the stairs.

Mary stood in the bay window looking every bit like a shop window fashion model in a simple slim fitting plain dress in her favourite colour of navy blue.

"For God's sake Mary, sit down, they won't get here any quicker with you jigging up and down in the window". Tony urged.

Once again Mary found herself staring impatiently from the lounge window looking across the neighbouring gardens towards the sea front for a glimpse of Gillian's car, and for no obvious reason she became concerned as she watched a string of bunting from one of the private guest houses had come adrift and was flying like a kite, tethered to the swinging B & B sign.

"Now you're beginning to make me nervous ..... sit down". Tony snapped, while at the same time joining her in the window. .

"They're here !" Mary squealed as she saw a red Fiesta turn off the promenade. Tony and Mary instinctively jumped back from view as Gillian's car rolled to a halt on the drive.

"Don't be so anxious, let them ring the bell". Tony requested. 'Waste of time' he thought to himself as Mary stood waiting in the open doorway with the strong wind scattering several sheets of paper from the desk throughout the hall.

"Mum". Gillian gasped excitedly.

"Come on in  quickly out of the cold". Mary interrupted.

"This is Jane. Jane, this is my mum". Gillian gushed ever more excited. Mary and Jane held and squeezed each others hands for several seconds before kissing each other in turn on the cheek.

"It's lovely to meet you Jane".

"I'm thrilled to meet you Missis Hooper, I've heard so much about you from Gillian". Jane said returning the greeting.

"Oh, not Missis Hooper, please call me Mary. Well Robert, what do you think about your lovely sister ?" Mary asked, feeling he was being slightly ignored. Robert smiled shyly and uttered quietly that he thought she was fantastic.

Not wanting to intrude on the initial family meeting Tony stayed in the background and stared from the lounge door at the slim pretty young woman dressed equally as stylish as Mary in a smart pale pink coloured two piece suit.

Still holding hands, Mary lead Jane along the hallway. "This is Tony, my longest and best friend". Tony gave Jane a hug and a kiss on the cheek. Gillian standing patiently waiting to enter the lounge cheekily whispered. "Bit more than friends. We'll tell you Tony's story later".

"Let's all get comfortable, I hope you haven't already eaten. Me and Jane are sitting on the settee". Mary stated emphatically, leading Jane by the hand around the obstructing coffee table.

"Squeeze up a bit mum, there's plenty of room for three". Gillian chirped. With Robert and Tony settled comfortably in an armchair each, Mary politely excused herself and promptly jumped from the settee.

"Gillian will you come and give me a hand for a minute". Mary requested as she headed for the kitchen. Instantly Mary returned and covered the coffee table with an orange coloured linen cloth, followed by Gillian precariously carrying two platters of sandwiches. Mary finally settled back after setting down a tray of teas on an adjacent occasional table.

"I think some plates would be useful". Tony remarked. Robert was the first to react and quickly returned with half a dozen medium size plates. "That's not enough, looking at the amount of food, we must be expecting a coach party on their way here". Tony joked.

Mary and Jane were engaged in deep conversation for several minutes complimenting each other on their choice of outfits until Gillian butted in. "Robert...tell us about meeting Jane at the airport".

Reluctantly Robert began. "There's not much to tell. I saw Jane's plane had landed and it seemed ages before she came through. I was beginning to think she wasn't on it, then I saw her and we instantly recognised each other from our photos. After we first said hello we went and had a cup of coffee and a chat".

"Oh come on, you must have hugged and kissed each other and cried a bit". Gillian jibed, trying to ring a bit more information from her husband.

"Of course we did but I'm not going to go into all that". Robert replied robustly.

"It was all very emotional, we ran to each other and held and kissed each other for ages before we decided to go to the cafeteria to and have a lovely chat". Jane intervened, noticing Robert's voice staring to quaver and his eyes beginning to water.

By now Mary and Gillian were also finding it difficult to control their emotions and began wiping away their tears.

"We stayed for about an hour in the café and then we caught a cab to the station. On the way home I told Jane all about my mum and dad, and Jane wants to go and meet mum. So we're going to go up later in the week. We also told each other our life stories on the train". Robert informed, having recovered his composure.

"Well we all know his". Gillian chirped and laughed. "Tell us about yourself Jane, tell us what happened to you, how did you come to be in Italy ?"

"I warn you it's not that interesting, just start yawning when you want me to stop". Jane joked.

"I don't remember all that much about living in South Africa, we had a tiny farm which mum had to run with the help of her father, my granddad. Dad would be around for a while then disappear for ages. My granddad went missing, mum later told me he'd been murdered. That was when dad arranged for us to come and live in England, mum said it wasn't safe for us in South Africa. This was a week before Christmas in nineteen eight two. He put us on the bus to the airport and said he'd be with us for Christmas but we never ever saw him again.

We lived in a flat, I can still visualise

the place. It was Horsham, near to the airport, It might be worth visiting, I can still picture the building and the inside of the flat, especially the landing".

"It's not far from where mum lives, we can go there when we visit her". Robert interrupted.

"Yes, I'd like to see if it's still there". Jane answered and then paused to drink the last drop of her tea. "Anyone ready for a yawn". Jane joked before continuing. "Me and mum spent that Christmas on our own. I know she started worrying when dad didn't show up and she must have been very worried not knowing who to contact. I don't even know whether we were legally in the country, thinking about it now.

Then Robert was born in the flat just after Christmas".

"I told you I was born in Horsham". Robert chipped in.

"I can remember mum telling me to go and knock on one of the flats on our landing to get some help. I was only seven. I was crying and frightened. One of the neighbours ran in to help mum and then called for an ambulance. Another lady came and looked after me when they took mum to hospital". Jane paused. "This must be getting a bit boring to listen to by now. I am going on a bit".

"No,…... in fact it's enthralling, please, please, carry on, it's fascinating". Mary insisted.

"Anyway, I'll try and cut it a bit short. Mum and the baby were rushed to hospital, then later on in the evening someone collected me and took me off somewhere. I don't know where but I hated it. It was a horrible place, I remember that much. I was taken to see mum a few times but I never saw the baby. And then they told me mum had died".

Mary could see that Jane was now crying and she put her arms around her shoulders to comfort her. Gillian handed Jane a tissue. "I'm sorry". Jane sighed heavily and wiped her eyes.

Mary looked sorrowfully at Jane as she tried to continue. "What was I going to say ? …… Oh yes, when they told me, I remember running out of the building and someone chased after me". Jane said while wiping away ever more tears that streamed across her cheeks.

"You poor girl, didn't anyone take care of you ?" Mary asked. Robert and Gillian were also now in tears and Tony sat in silence, spellbound, occasionally wiping his eyes when he assumed no one could see.

"They took me to mum's funeral, there was only two other people there, I've never been able to find out where she was buried. Then I seem to spend my life in and out of different foster homes. One couple were very nice but they kept moving me on and I think the others were only interested in the money they got for having me.

My first memory of England was when I was seven and landing at Heathrow. I remember dreaming about being an air hostess after seeing the smart girls on the plane. So as soon as I left school I applied for a job there. I had a letter back listing several vacancies, no hostesses. I finished up working in the cafeteria, and that's where I met Gianni. He was studying law in London and every Monday and Friday he always stopped for coffee. We got chatting, he said I helped him with his English. Then he asked me out, and when I was eighteen we got married in Rome and I've lived there ever since".

Mary and Gillian simultaneously gave out an enormous sigh. "How romantic, what a lovely fairy tail ending".

"Meeting Robert and spending time in that café brought back all those memories".

"Do you speak Italian ?" Gillian asked.

"I can, just about, it was difficult to learn. I did go to evening language class but mostly I picked it up from Gianni.

"Do you work ?" Gillian again quizzed.

"I do, but it's mainly just to keep me busy, I have a job as a guide with the tourist board. I take Italian and English speaking holiday groups around Rome. I'm the lady with the coloured umbrella. This time of year there's not a lot going on so I can have as much time away as I want".

"What does Gianni do ?" Gillian again questioned.

"He's a lawyer with a large firm in Rome". Jane answered proudly.

"The name of your villa sounds very grand". Gillian again chipped in with another question.

"I think all Italian names sound grand. No it's just a typical slightly run down terrace building. It was left to Gianni when his mother died about five years ago. His parents were divorced a long while ago, I never met his father. We've lived there since we got married". Jane concluded with a long sigh of relief. "And that's about it".

"Jane". Gillian called cheekily, and then pointed to the mysterious lady on the wedding photograph that she'd purposely had printed. "It's not very clear but we thought the lady's face could have been you, she does look a bit like you", Jane joined in the laughter. "I wish I had known about the wedding, I would love to say it is me. I'd have loved to be at your wedding".

"It calls for a drink now" Mary stated and instructed Tony to fetch some glasses. With everyone holding their glass filled with champagne Tony made a short sincere speech welcoming Jane. "A toast! To Jane and Robert". He announced. "To Jane and Robert". He repeated with Mary and Gillian.

"That's given you something to put in your scrapbook towards this story you're trying to write". Tony commented.

++++++++++++

## Chapter Thirteen

"Well that was a fascinating evening, she's certainly a lovely young lady. How she got through that story I don't know, it was heart breaking at times". Mary recalled as she placed Tony's breakfast on the pine kitchen table.

"Robert was the lucky sibling, at least he had a good mother, and now he's got a great sister. You never told Jane how we first met". Tony muttered.

"I completely forgot, Gillian must have forgotten as well. Mind you, Gillian will have told her herself by now, knowing our Gillian". Mary replied. "She's a cheeky devil, kept on asking Jane one question after another, and then suggesting she was the girl in the photo". She added. "That's Gillian". Tony quipped.

"I've got a few things to see to, so I'm going to nip off home when I've finished my breakfast. You watch ... your neighbour next door always manages to appear out front and says good morning to me whenever I stay over for the night". Tony chirped.

"She's alright, she's good fun, she always has a bit of banter with me, asking when we're going to get married". Mary replied.

"Well when are we then ?" Tony asked optimistically.

"You know the answer to that, now bugger off and do whatever it is you've got to do and I'll see you later". Mary quipped.

"These Tuesdays come round ever so quick, it'll be Christmas before we know it". Mary uttered as she climbed into Tony's Mercedes. "Gillian phoned me this morning, they'd just arrived at Robert's mother's bungalow". Mary added.

"I didn't realise they were going today, no one said anything". Tony retorted.

"I didn't know either, Gillian said they only decided last night on the spur of the moment. She's going to give me another call this evening to let me know how they got on". Mary replied.

Tony and Mary joined a small group of regular tea dancers in the hotel car park, all making their way to the ballroom. Les the keyboard player thanked Tony for his entrance money and carried on playing for several couples already on the dance floor. Tony skirted around the edge of the floor to their usual table while Mary was in constant demand to discuss the arrival of Jane, pausing at each table, and eventually re-joining Tony just as Les announced the interval waltz.

"Sorry Tony, but everyone wanted to know all about Robert's sister. Are you fed up ?".

"No...why should I be ? I've had a dance with Alma and a couple of dances with the Jenkin twins". Tony answered.

"Are you sure that you actually danced with both of them ?" Mary joked.

"Very funny...I'll fetch some drinks".

"Well as for dancing, this afternoon was a waste of time for me". Mary moaned as Tony quickly closed the front door to preserve the warmth from the hall. Mary tossed her top coat through the open lounge door on to the nearest chair and entered the kitchen. "I'll make a pot of tea, dinner will be about an hour". She called out to Tony, now stood gazing in the hall mirror combing his wind blown greying hair.

"I'm just popping to the bathroom, I'll drop your coat on the bed". He said, peering into the kitchen.

"Your tea's on the table going cold". Mary screeched from the bottom of the staircase. "How much longer are you going to be, I've prepared all the vegetables and put the dinner on to cook while you've been up there preening yourself". A clearly irritated Mary added.

"I daresay you've cut the grass and

repainted the bloody house as well". Tony muttered jokingly under his breath as he descended the stairs.

"I heard that !" Mary snapped.

"God, I hope you're not going to be in this mood all evening, has it got something to do with the dance ? The phone's ringing let's hope it's Gillian with some news to cheer you up".

"Yes Gillian how did you get on, are you back home ?" Mary asked before her daughter had chance to speak.

"No mum, we've booked into a hotel in Horsham for the night. We ran out of time, we stayed at Robert's mum's bungalow until three o'clock and then went on to find the flat where Robert was born".

"How did Jane and his mum get on ?"

"They got on wonderful together, that's why we stayed so long. Robert and his mum were fine as well. It was the first time he'd seen her since he'd known about his adoption. So now everything is happily sorted".

"Oh that's good. Did you manage to find the flat ?" Mary asked.

"Yes, it's still there, the whole block had recently been refurbished". Gillian paused for a moment to listen to Jane.

"I can hear Jane, what's she saying ?" Mary interrupted.

"She's telling me to tell you that we met the actual lady who helped her mum".

"Wow, that's amazing, she still lives there then ?" Mary replied with a hint of surprise in he voice.

"It was all very exciting mum, Jane managed to ring the correct bell first time. Missis Simpson, that's this lady, didn't believe who Jane was at first, eventually Jane proved it to her and she invited us up to her flat. She told us someone had called on her just over a year ago asking questions about Missis Stewart and Jane assumes that must have been the people from Worldwide". Gillian paused for a second time to catch her breath.

"We thought it was fantastic that she still lived there, she said she'd been living in the same flat since they were built. She remembered Jane's mum and Jane crying outside her door just before Christmas".

"What did she say about Jane's mum, did she mention her husband ?" Mary asked.

"She said she only spoke to her half a dozen times but she said she seemed a nice lady. She never saw a man at the flat.

Robert thinks the owners of the flat might still have some old records. Missis Simpson gave us the details of the letting agents. She said they'd never changed, So we're going to their offices in the morning. Robert's already made an appointment, he's hoping to find some information about their dad. He thinks it must have been his dad who organised the lease and they still have a record of it. So we're going there at nine in the morning. And now we're going to enjoy the evening in this posh hotel. I'll ring after our meeting, bye mum. Robert and Jane are saying bye".

"Yes... I can hear them Gill, bye".

"I hope you heard all that". Mary cried as Tony replaced the hall handset.

"Well they seem to have had an exciting day, I think Robert will be a bit disappointed tomorrow at this meeting. I can't imagine the agents having or wanting to even spend time searching through years old records". Tony remarked doubtfully.

A pale shaft of early morning sunlight sneaked through a gap in the curtains casting a tapered strip of light as far as the bed. Mary crossed the floor from her bed and drew back the curtains to reveal the start of another cold cheerless day. The watery sunshine attempting to raise the temperature. "I suppose I'll have to do my monthly shop today, or starve !" Mary said, talking to herself as she descended the stairs.

"Morning Beryl". Mary called across to her neighbour, at the same time struggling to close her garage door.

"Morning Mary, it's a cold one this morning". Beryl shouted back as both ladies approached each other either side of the garden wall. After ten minutes of hilarious conversation and with both ladies beginning to fidget to keep warm, Mary resisted the temptation to extend the discussion.

"I must go, I've left my engine running. Come round when I get back, I'll tell you all about Gillian's new sister-in-law".

A bemused Missis Parker watched Mary reverse into the road and drive away.

Mary returned from her once a month trip to the out of town supermarket, having taken the usual hour and three quarters. Always parking in the same bay and racing around the aisles collecting exactly the same goods she always buys. A repetitive exercise always culminating at the check out with the shortest queue.

After three trips to and from the car she was out of the cold with her bags of groceries standing on the floor in the hall.

"Oh God..Beryl give me chance to get in". Mary chuntered to herself as she shuffled past her shopping to answer the door. "Come in Beryl". She invited not too convincingly. Beryl steered her way past the shopping and on into the kitchen.

"Put the kettle on Beryl and make some tea while I get my frozen stuff put away".

"I hope I haven't come round too soon, but you've got me curious about Gillian's sister. I didn't know you had another daughter". Beryl called out above the noise of filling the kettle.

"I haven't, I thought I said her sister-in-law". Mary replied. "The rest of the bags can stay for a while. Let's take our tea in the lounge, it's a bit warmer in there".

Beryl listened intently as Mary told the whole story of Gillian's husband finding out about his adoption and the fascinating events leading to the discovery that he now has a sister living in Italy, and that she's here, and at the moment the three of them are visiting the place were Robert was born. Mary began to enlarge on the details when she was interrupted by the sound of the door bell.

Mary stood bewildered in the open doorway, surprised to be confronted by two uniformed lady police officers. "Are you Missis Hooper ?" The elder and more senior of the two officers presumed.

"Yes". Mary replied hesitantly.

"Do you mind if we come inside ?"

"I'll get out of your way Mary, I'll see you later". Beryl announced as she squeezed past in the hallway.

Mary was now too fearful and concerned to even glance at the officer's identifications. "Is Gillian Hooper related to yourself?" The senior lady officer politely enquired.

"She's my daughter". Mary replied nervously almost anticipating the follow up words from the officer. "What's wrong, has something happened to her?" She blurted out anxiously.

"We've been contacted by the Reigate Constabulary that she has been involved in a motor accident". Seeing that Mary was looking faint, the youngest officer guided her to a chair. "Don't worry". She commented before Mary asked the question again. "She is in hospital but she's going to be fine, her injuries aren't life threatening".

These words of comfort did not ease Mary's fears. "Are you sure she is going to be alright, what happened, is she badly injured ..... Is she?" Mary begged for more positive information.

"At the moment we've only been told that she hasn't any life threatening injuries". The senior officer replied sympathetically.

"What about her husband and his sister, are they alright?" Mary asked.

"As far as we know she was alone in the car".

"I don't understand, they were all together, how do you know if it is my daughter ?" Mary cried.

"Apparently the only identification the Reigate police had was her driving license they found in the car". The senior officer replied.

"But I still don't understand why she was driving on her own". Mary repeated.

"Do you have Gillian's husband's phone number ?"

Mary could feel the blood pumping in her chest as she collected an address book from the desk in the hall. "That's Robert's number". She advised holding the book. open.

"Would you like me to speak to him ?" The officer asked.

Mary pondered for a moment. "I'll be fine in a minute, I think I ought to phone him myself". "Hello ... Robert".

"It's Jane Mary, I've got his phone, I left mine at their house. Robert has Gillian's. What's the matter you sound upset".

"Yes I am, where's Robert ?"

"He's just gone back to the letting agents car park. Gillian drove away on her own, he's gone to see if she's come back. there. Oh he's just crossing the road, what's the matter, are you alright ?" Jane urged.

"Don't panic, she's had an accident, she's alright". Mary said calmly.

"Oh God". Jane squealed as Robert snatched the phone from her hand.

"Who's this ? Oh it's you Mary, what's the matter ?" Robert snapped.

"Gillian has been in an accident, she is okay, don't worry". Mary stressed..

"How do you know ?" Robert asked with the accent on the word 'you'. "What has happened ?" He added anxiously.

"I've got two police ladies here with me. She is in hospital but she's alright. Why was she on her own. What's going on ?" Mary insisted.

"We had a bit of an upset at the agent's and she left the office. By the time me and Jane got outside the car had gone. We've been hanging around near their car park for the past two hours waiting for her to come back. Are you telling me the truth, she isn't badly hurt ?"

"That's what the police have told me". Mary replied.

"Which hospital is she in ?" Robert asked. "Do you know which hospital she's been taken to ?" Mary asked the lady officers. After a short pause. "You need to ring the police at Reigate, have you got a pen and paper ?" Mary then proceeded to read the number being displayed by the officer.

"Why did they call on you ?" Robert asked.

"Gillian's driving license was in the glove compartment, and it's still in her own name and this address". Mary uttered.

Jane regained possession of Robert's phone. "Robert's getting a bit upset, you're sure she is going to be alright ?"

"I can only tell you what the police have told me, you need to get over to the hospital". Mary instructed.

"Robert's ringing the police number now". Jane replied.

"What made her decide to go off on her own, tell me, what's going on ?" Mary again asked.

"They had quite an upset in the letting agents, Robert will tell you all about it later. He's just said she's here in Crawley hospital, now he's popping back to the agent's office to find a number for a taxi. Was there anyone else hurt ?" Jane added.

Mary mouthed the question to the senior officer. "No, apparently there wasn't any other car involved".

"I'll ring you later from the hospital, this could be our taxi. Bye".

The two lady police officers shook hands with Mary as they departed, leaving her alone in the house anxiously awaiting news from the hospital, Mary watched from the window as the police car moved away. Then hastily stepped back from view and peered from behind the curtain as Beryl and her husband drove on to their driveway, hoping she hadn't attracted her neighbour's attention.

Mary nervously wandered from room to room with one eye constantly on the time. She watched as the hands on the clock rotated ....three....four...five...six o'clock and still Mary waited now with the telephone handset firmly gripped in her right hand willing it to ring. Mary decided in her mind that she would wait another hour and then contact the hospital herself.

"I hope Beryl doesn't decide to pop back round". She sighed out loud, knowing her neighbour's inquisitive nature.

Although anticipating a call, the harsh piercing ring of the telephone, still held in her hand startled Mary, causing her to fumble trying to locate the receive button. "It's Jane Mary, Sorry we've took so long to call, but we've only just been allowed to see her".

"How is she ?" Mary butted in, her voice stuttering, fearing Jane's reply.

"Stop worrying Mary. She is going to be alright". Jane replied trying to assure her. "She's in the intensive care unit at the moment, they've just brought her back from having an x-ray. The nurse has just told us that she's fractured her sternum and broken three ribs. She's heavily sedated at the moment, and first thing tomorrow she's having an operation to remove one of her ribs that they fear could puncture her lung"

A period of silence prevailed before Mary could reply. "That doesn't sound very good, what if something happens to her in the night, and what about her chest bone ?".

"Nothing will happen, stop worrying she is going to be alright". Jane answered sympathetically.

"Is Robert okay ?" Mary enquired.

"He's alright Mary, he's just gone to fetch some drinks".

"Why did she drive off". Mary asked once again.

"I'd sooner Robert tell you. He"ll see you sometime, tomorrow, we're staying here for another night now. We're going to stay until Gillian's had her operation".

Knowing that Mary was not going to let go in her quest for an answer, Jane apologised and ended the call.  .

Mary found herself sitting in total darkness gazing through the lounge window at a faulty street lamp flickering furiously until it's light extinguished altogether. Her mind was so occupied with her daughter's situation that she didn't realise that Tony had entered the house and standing in the lounge doorway.

"Mary …. What on earth are you doing in the dark ? And it's freezing in here".

"Oh my God, you frightened the life out of me. Why didn't you ring ?" Mary snapped sharply.

"I did ring, then I used my key. I thought there was something wrong. What's the matter with you ?" Tony demanded to know. "Let me pop your heating on and draw the curtains".

"It's Gillian, I've had an awful day". Mary replied and then spent the next half an hour recalling the eventful day.

"Has anyone said how the accident happened ?" Tony asked.

"Not yet, I daresay we'll find out from the police tomorrow, they must have taken the car away by now. They're going to stay with Gillian as long as they can, then catching the train. Jane's going to ring me after Gillian's had her operation. For some reason Robert doesn't want to speak to me. I keep asking why she was on her own but Jane won't say. She says Robert will tell me. Something's gone on between them".

"Why don't we drive up there early in the morning. We can see Gillian ourselves and bring Jane and Robert home". Tony suggested.

"It would be a great relief to see her, are you sure you want to drive all that way ?"

"Ring Jane now and tell her we'll be there about ten. Get the address of the hospital. I'm just going out to fill the car. When you've done that how about some dinner, I'm starving". Tony responded.

Mary woke up as Tony located a place in the hospital car park and switched off the engine, then repositioned his seat to give maximum room.

"What time is it ?" Mary asked with a stifled yawn.

"It's ten past eleven, took longer to get here than I expected". Tony replied while stretching his legs under the bulkhead.

"Which way to the hospital entrance ?" Mary asked in desperate need to visit the toilets.

Once inside they both disappeared to their respective toilets. Mary returned to find Tony studying a colourful hospital floor plan. After leaving the lift at the appropriate floor level, followed by a hesitant wander along the corridor Tony declared. "This is it". And immediately pressed the white plastic security button mounted to the side of the double width doors. "Hello, can I help you?" "Yes please, we're here to visit Gillian Hines, she was admitted yesterday. It's her mother and a friend". "Push the door and come on through". The voice instructed.

Jane came part way along the short corridor to intercept Mary and Tony and without saying a word they followed her to Gillian's bedside.

Mary carefully leaned across the bed and kissed her daughter on the forehead. Then standing and staring from the bottom of the bed was horrified at the extent of the bruising to Gillian's eyes and face.

"She's not long come back from the operating theatre, the sister has only just brought her round". Jane informed.

"She looks very tired. How do you feel Gillian?" Mary asked, instantly realising the futility of such a question. Gillian tried to brave a smile but remained silent.

The ward sister returned to be present as the doctor approached and introduced himself. Immediately Robert engaged him in a whispered conversation.

"What is Robert asking the doctor?" Mary asked Jane, also in a hushed voice.

"He told me last night that Gillian is pregnant so I think he's probably asking if the baby is alright". Jane replied. Mary smiled at this news and as soon as

Robert concluded his conversation with the doctor. Mary asked. "And is the baby alright ?" Robert just answered with an abrupt "yes" but didn't appear to be any happier or offer any further explanation. Mary felt a bit upset by his attitude but put it down to his concern for Gillian and decided not to say anything further for the time being.

The doctor concluded his thorough examination of Gillian and after a few words of assurance he move on to the adjacent patient.

"Robert's just been telling me, the police were here this morning but they weren't allowed to see Gillian but they told Robert that a witness statement from a car that was following Gillian said that she just went off the road and into a drainage ditch. They said they couldn't see any reason why, they thought she may have fallen asleep at the wheel or fainted". Tony said and added. "They've given Robert the name and address of the garage that recovered the car".

"Have Robert and Gillian had a row ?" Mary whispered to Jane still in pursuit of a reason for Gillian to drive off alone.

"No, nothing like that, honestly Mary, don't ask me, it's not my business, Robert will tell you". Jane pleaded.

"How long has Robert known about

the baby ?" Mary asked.

"Only a few days, he told me last night at the hotel". Jane replied as Tony and Robert stood still deep in conversation.

"The nurse would like us to leave now, she thinks we ought to let Gillian get some rest". Robert said relaying her wishes.

"She has gone back to sleep so we might as well make tracks". Tony suggested.

The long tedious drive home was mainly in silence. Mary from time to time attempted to engage Robert in conversation, hoping he would reveal what had happened at the letting agents. After leaving Robert and Jane, Mary was thankful to arrive back home, having relieved Tony and driven the latter half of the journey in darkness.

"Who'd have thought it, a week ago I was wondering if I would ever become a grandma, and now I'm going to have two beautiful grandchildren next year".

+++++++++++

## Chapter Fourteen

"It's been a couple of weeks since we fetched Gillian from the hospital, has she said anything about the accident yet?" Tony asked.

"Neither of them have mentioned it, or said anything about the baby to me. I know a nurse calls to see her twice a week, so she is being looked after". Mary replied fretfully. "She's on her own today, I'd like to pop over and see her. Robert's off to Reigate this morning to collect the car, their neighbour took him to the station".

"It's a pity Jane couldn't stay on to keep Gillian company". Tony said.

"She's coming back in a couple of weeks time with her husband and staying over for Christmas. Shall we get going to Gillian's?". Mary replied

It was obvious to Mary that Gillian was still in a great deal of pain when she opened the cottage door. "Oh ... hello mum, Tony, I wasn't expecting you. Robert's gone to get my car".

"Yes we know, Thomas told me, any idea how long he'll be?" Mary asked.

"He's just phoned me from Winchester, he's stopped to get something to eat. He reckons he'll be home by seven".

"Your pain's not getting any better". Mary stated as she observed her daughter wincing while helping her back to her chair.

"It is a bit better, as long as I don't go and forget and cough or take a deep breath".

"Anyway young lady, are you going to tell me what the problem is with you and Robert ? Everything seemed perfect before you went to see the flat". Mary requested, instantly causing Gillian to start crying.

Mary put an arm around Gillian's shoulder. "Tell me, what is it, what has happened ?". Mary pleaded sympathetically, only to cause Gillian to clutch her chest and cry even harder.

Through her tears and to evade her mother's inquisition Gillian stuttered. "I've a hospital appointment on Monday, will you take me to avoid Robert having to ask for any more time off ?"

"Yes of course I will. But tomorrow, you and Robert are coming to dinner. I mean it, you will come ! And you'll tell me what's going on with the pair of you". Mary snapped emphatically. "Gillian and Robert are coming over to us tomorrow". Mary informed Tony as he emerged from the tiny kitchen with three mugs of coffee, at the same time giving Gillian an instructive glare. "Tomorrow !". Mary stressed aggressively.

Robert supported Gillian as she painfully struggled to get out of the repaired Fiesta. Mary met them on the drive and together with Robert helped her into the house. Tony waited in the hall and carefully assisted Gillian with removing her coat and guided her into the lounge and into his own favourite armchair. Robert occupied the opposing chair nervously clutching some folded papers.

"I've just had a look at the Fiesta, they must have done a good job, The car looks brand new". Tony commented in Robert's direction.

"They told me the damage was to the offside and the front. They said they had to fit a new door, a new wing and bonnet, front fender and all new lighting and some interior work. Door panel and dash". Robert moaned dolefully.

Mary appeared from the kitchen and set a tray of teas on to the coffee table and dropped into the settee alongside Tony.

"Right now then you two. No more avoiding the issue. I know there's something wrong. What's been going on ?" Mary demanded.

Gillian looked across towards Robert sheepishly. "You're not going to be very pleased mum".

"I'll decide that, let's hear it". Mary abruptly interrupted.

"Me and Robert are brother and sister. We've got the same father". Gillian blurted out and instantly burst into uncontrollable sobbing. Mary and Tony looked at each other in amazement.

"Don't be stupid Gillian, where's this nonsense come from?" Mary snapped angrily.

Robert stood from his chair and handed Mary the papers he'd been nursing. "These are photo copies the letting agents gave us. The lady at the agents had these details of the original lease to the flat ready as soon as we got to their office. She said she had two brothers living in that block of flats so she was interested to search through the archives".

"Well what are these papers supposed to tell me?" Mary again snapped, showing signs of irritation.

"Read the bloody things, or listen to Robert". Gillian retaliated robustly then wiped the water from her face.

"I thought that my dad would have taken out the lease for mum and he would have had to have a witness, and if the witness was still around I might be able to find out something about dad. The witness is usually a friend or a colleague".

By now Tony and Mary were deeply engrossed in the documents. "This says the lease in the name of K J Stewart. So what's the problem ?" Mary interjected.

"Yes we know that ! But look at the other document, this was attached to the lease, and look at the name on the rent and the deposit receipt .... Thomas Hooper !"

Mary and Tony were momentarily stunned into silence. Mary suddenly felt her blood pressure begin to rise and her face feeling hot and flushed.

'It's obviously another Thomas Hooper". She insisted.

"Maybe it is, but is that his signature on the lease ? and why is his name down as Thomas Barnes on my birth certificate ? Why not Thomas Hooper ?" Robert requested.

"Well we're certain it is our dad, so we're going to have to get a separation, and I've had a word at the hospital about an early termination. I am sorry mum, but there's no other way". Gillian cried.

"Even if it was my Thomas, he wasn't your father". Mary screeched loudly. Tony sat and stared anxiously at Mary, anticipating her next words. "Tony is your dad !" She said defiantly. "So now at last you know". Mary added and sighed heavily with the relief that their twenty five year secret was ended.

"I don't believe you mum. You're just saying this to keep us together". Gillian snorted and began crying again.

"Gillian .... Do you think I'd want it to continue if you were brother and sister ?" Mary replied forcefully. "No ! off course I wouldn't". She answered herself and then turned her anger on to Tony, kicking his shin. "You bloody well say something, instead of just sitting there". She snapped.

"Why didn't you tell me this years ago, I'd have loved for Tony to be my dad".

"Despite what everybody said, I've always had a sneaky feeling my husband would come back one day and then what would I have done, and I didn't want to spoil your relationship with Thomas and Daniel. Tony's yearned for the day to let you know he's your dad, just a pity it had to be like this". Mary concluded and flopped exhausted back onto the settee the side of Tony. "In secret he's always been your dad. Now look, he's in tears !". Mary added, placing her arm around his shoulders.

"I can see all that now, he was always the one to play with me when I was little and he always came to the school with you, and he's been so generous to me, and to Robert". Gillian commented as the tears of joy traced across her cheeks.

"My dad must be the same Thomas Hooper". Robert interjected. "My mum lived in South Africa and we know he worked there all through the troubles in the seventies and the early eighties. It can't be a coincidence".

"I'll have a look for his signature. Just a thought, in the attic there should be a plastic container with all his overseas expenses, bank statements, cheque stubs and other stuff. Daniel put it up there years ago. I don't know what you could find, I've no idea where it is. It's a largish box, I think it's clear plastic".

Before anyone could blink, Robert was bounding up the stairs and within a few minutes the noise of the attic ladder being lowered was apparent.

"You look a lot better now Gillian". Mary stated, observing her daughter's face smiling through her tears for the first time in weeks.

"I am, I've no pain, well praps' just a bit. Move up dad". Gillian replied joyously and squeezed in between Tony and Mary on the settee. Tony wiped away his tears and cuddled his daughter for the first time since she was a baby, and overjoyed to hear her call him 'dad'.

Mary then carefully explained their parentage, that Robert's parents were Thomas Hooper or Barnes and his mother was Katherine Stewart. And that Tony and herself were her mum and dad and that there wasn't any blood line between them whatsoever. "Right now we're all back as one big happy family, I'll check on the dinner. It's a casserole".

"Robert !!". Tony shouted into the attic. "Dinner's on the table".

"Leave him up there. Shut the lid". Gillian joked.

"I'll have another look after dinner". Robert announced as he descended the stairs brushing away the cobwebs.

For the second time within an hour Robert cleared away the cobwebs and dusted himself off. "You found it then". Mary stated. "I'll have a good look for something with his signature on later".

"Can I take the box with me or we'll be here all night looking through this lot". Robert asked. "We need to get going, you ready Gill ?"

Gillian gave Tony a loving hug and a daughter's kiss. "Bye dad, bye mum".

"Go on, before you have me crying again". Tony quipped.

++++++++++++

# Chapter Fifteen

On this chilly Saint Valentines morning Mary and Tony stood facing the lady registrar and listened to her words. "I now pronounce you husband and wife. You may kiss your bride".

Seated in the small registry office, the immediate family including Jane and her handsome Italian husband Gianni, and a few close friends, erupted into rapturous applause as the lady registrar made the announcement, and continued clapping as the couple walked holding hands to the rear of the room.

The mid morning wedding was followed by a brunch style reception meal a few minutes walk away at the Knoll House Hotel.

"Speech...speech" A familiar voice well known to Tony cried out.

"Okay Susan". Tony laughed as he got to his feet receiving a pat on his shoulder from Mary. I haven't prepared any notes so I won't bore you, it'll be short. I'd just like to say that this Christmas just gone has given me the best presents I could ever wish for. I've got my daughter Gillian, and a complete family who've treated me as a family member for the past twenty five years. And at long last Mary accepted my proposal of marriage. And to top it all, I'm going to be a granddad. I want to thank Gillian for giving her mother to me and Thomas for being my best man. And for all of you for this reception and your lovely presents. And last but by no means least of all......my sister-in-law Susan for recalling all those memories from fifty years ago". Tony concluded.

"It's just a pity it wasn't you knocking on our door instead of the other lad. But you got the girl in the end". Susan replied followed by another spontaneous round of applause.

Tony sat down only to quickly jump back. "As you all know we're off on our cruise tomorrow, so we'll be leaving you all in half an hour to drive to our hotel in Southampton. The bar bill's paid and you've got the room till three, so enjoy a drink or two on us. Cheers everyone". Tony added as he raised his glass.

"Southampton my bum !". Susan joked, sending Gillian and Mary into a fit of laughter. "Gillian …. Susan thinks your dad looks just like Rossano Brazzi, do you think so ?" Mary asked in a hushed voice. "I don't know, who's Rossano Brazzi ?" "Oh, never mind". Mary replied in despair.

Along with all their guests Tony and Mary waited and watched as Daniel drove

Tony's Mercedes round to the hotel main entrance. "Look at the state of that, that's Susan and Gillian for you". Tony exclaimed, as everyone laughed at the array of tacky messages, balloons and tin cans attached to the vehicle. "That lots coming off as soon as we're out of sight. I hope no ones messed with our suitcases .... Susan ?" Tony shouted as he playfully tapped her on the back of her head before giving her a kiss on the cheek. "Have a lovely honeymoon, and don't get lost on the way to Southampton. You know what I mean". Susan chirped.

"I know we've come along the coast for a nicer ride but why have you turned down this road". Mary asked suspiciously as Tony steered the car around the island just before Wareham town centre. After a further ten minutes the ruins of Corfe Castle perched above the road came into view. "You're going to Swanage, you romantic old sod". Mary quipped. "I hope you've allowed enough time to get to Southampton".

Tony remained silent as he drove up the winding road between the Purbeck stone cottages and on through the village and arriving in Swanage fifteen minutes later, passing the railway station and following the road round and stopping a hundred yards from the pier. "We're surely not going on the pier". Mary stated as she grappled with her top coat after leaving the warmth of the car. "Have we really got time to hang around ?" Mary asked as they climbed the steps and walked hand in hand to the end of the pier.

"This is the very spot where we caught up with you and Susan fifty years ago. We'd followed you all the way from the amusement arcade". Tony said as they leaned on the ornate railings looking across water in the fading light at the sweep of the shoreline. .

"I remember it well, it was either give in or jump off the pier". Mary joked.

"The pier wasn't as deserted then as it is now, there's only one other couple on here. They must be as daft as us". She added.

"Are we going to get to our hotel in time for our meal, I'm starving now ?" Mary asked.

"This was meant to be my surprise. I thought you would have guessed from Susan's comments. We're staying here tonight, we've got plenty of time to get to Southampton tomorrow morning. There's a Valentine's dinner dance tonight in the hotel I chose, I thought you'd like that". Tony replied. Mary didn't answer but smiled at Tony curiously as a melody began to play seemingly out from nowhere. Tony began miming to the song emanating from inside his coat pocket. "Some enchanted evening. you may see a stranger...you may see a stranger across a crowded.........." Mary thought to herself. 'Is this just a romantic coincidence or does he know something', then as the music continued and Tony stopped pretending to be the singer, a stupid grin appeared on his face.

"You silly bugger". Mary whispered affectionately, but slightly embarrassed at noticing the other couple had wandered into listening range.

++++++++++

# Chapter Sixteen

Looking back towards the docked cruise liner on which they'd just spent the last twenty one days, already being prepared for it's evening departure, Tony and Mary slowly made their way from the dockside to the waiting vehicle to return them to the car storage compound.

Tony sighed with relief as the engine immediately burst into life and after a few minutes to set the satnav he guided the Mercedes out into the busy morning traffic.

Mary's house, their future home was a welcome sight after an arduous four hour traffic laden journey, and to see Gillian's red Fiesta parked on the drive added to their delight.

"How long have you been waiting ?" Mary asked Gillian the moment the door opened.

"I've been here since twelve, I came to pop your heating on and to bring you some groceries". Gillian replied and watched Tony huddle up to the radiator as soon as he entered the hallway. "That's three weeks in the sunshine for you". Gillian quipped.

After half an hour of holiday recollections and a cup of tea, Gillian finally grabbed the opportunity to speak. "Anyway....That plastic box....Robert finally found a bank statement. I intended to bring it but I forgot, but there's a payment dated November the tenth, nineteen eighty two to the letting agents for the exact same amount as the deposit for the flat". Gillian paused to allow a reaction from her mother.

"I can't argue with that then, can I? But it wouldn't really have mattered anyway because you know your dad is Tony". Mary replied, and now quietly felt justified for her initial affair with Tony when Thomas was away. "That's all over now, how are you and Robert, you certainly look a lot better". Mary stated.

"I'm out of pain at last, one more hospital visit, that's all". Gillian replied. "Oh Robert's okay now he's all sorted and Jane and Gianni went back last Monday. They've asked us to visit them for a holiday".

"A Roman holiday, that sounds lovely, and are you going?" Mary asked.

"We're going in the Easter holiday break". Gillian replied excitedly.

"Will you be alright, how are those ribs now? And how is my grandchild?"

"I really am feeling fine mum, and I'm still five months away, Debra's will be your first".

Tony emerged from the kitchen with a plate in each hand. "So you and Robert are off to Italy". He commented and whispered quietly to Gillian.

"What's he offered you ?" Mary asked.

"Dad just said that you two will pay our flight".

"Well if that's what he said you'd better get booked up". Mary chirped.

"I'm going to get off home now mum, there's some mail on the desk, and Missis Parker popped round while I was here with a package. It was too big to go through the letter box. It's with your mail".

"We'll call round in the week to bore you with our photos". Tony called out as Gillian reached her car.

"Oh, I nearly forgot, there's a cottage pie in the oven, it needs cooking. Bye"

Tony retrieved their luggage from the Mercedes and dumped it in the hallway. "That can stay there till tomorrow". He said as he picked up the mail from the desk and dropped it on to the pine kitchen table in front of Mary.

After discarding all but three letters Mary mused the package suspiciously. "This seems a bit official, it's stamped 'Foreign Office'. And so is this letter. I wonder which came first and if they're connected".

"The letter's dated earlier than the package, so I'd open the letter first". Tony suggested. Mary shuddered as she read the heading 'Ref; Thomas Hooper (deceased)' "This letter is telling me that they will be forwarding me the property of the above person in the next ten days". Mary choked nervously. "Well this must be it, You open it". She added.

Tony sat back down besides Mary after collecting a sharp kitchen knife and removed the contents. "It's his leather folder he used to carry his note book and all his documents. It's in a bit of a mess". Mary added as Tony removed the folder from it's plastic carrier, releasing an official covering letter. And then undid one of the two press stud fasteners, the other being broken, to reveal the items inside. "This letter says the item was found by a farmer in Turkey when he was ploughing a field but was only handed over to the Turkish authorities a year ago. This was after the old farmer had died and his son inherited the farm and found the folder in a barn". Tony remarked, briefly describing the letter.

Meanwhile Mary spread out the daily newspaper on the kitchen table. "Put it on here". She instructed Tony as he carefully looked inside for any contents.

"Whoever killed him took most of his details, there's no passport and not a lot else either. Plenty dried up soil". Tony uttered.

"You open that, I'm not touching that envelope. Whoever killed him has probably held it". Mary squirmed. "I can see some writing on the envelope". She added and flinched again.

"I think that says Fort Victoria. That's in South Africa, or it used to be. It's called something else now". Tony informed.

"What's inside ?" Mary snapped. Tony carefully opened the delicate envelope and removed two water marked monochrome photographs, and laid one of them face up on the newspaper, temporary withholding the other.

"Well that's not bloody well me". Mary snapped harshly at the sight of a beautiful young woman staring back at her. "Do you think it's Robert's mum ?" Mary added.

"I don't know, but look at this one". Tony said and laid the other picture on the paper.

"Oh my God, if that is Robert's mum ...... this looks like a hospital portrait taken in a maternal ward. If the one baby is Jane, who is the other ?" Mary squealed.

"Read the writing on the back of the first photo, it's just about readable". Tony urged and flipped it over.

"To my darling Thomas  Love Kathy xxxx". Mary read out aloud. "And to think I've felt guilty for being with you. Is there anything on the other one". She added as Tony turned it over. Mary still refusing to touch anything.

"It seems to have a studio stamp on it and dated. Looks like 'Fort V' or could be 'Port'. And I assume that would be a telephone number if you could see all of it. The date is something ending in a six". Tony remarked. "Shall I give Robert a ring, he'll want to see these".

"I'll ring Gillian tomorrow it's a bit late now. We don't want him shooting round here this time of night". Mary replied.

Mary squirmed as Tony removed the remaining contents from the folder and laid them out on the newspaper, together with a dusting of dried up dirt and bits of withered old wheat. "That's about it, this looks as if it could have been his work permit, hardly readable. And a couple of sheets of paper with some scribble notes, if you could read them, it's probably part of his report about something or other. This is the only thing with any detail that I can just about make out, this looks like a medical card".

Tony put the two photos to one side and carefully returned the remaining pieces of partly disintegrated papers to the folder as Mary looked on horrified.

+++++++++++

## Chapter Seventeen

"I've rung Gillian, they're coming round as soon as Robert gets home. And Susan phoned me while you were out". Mary remarked.

"How's your mother ?" Tony enquired.

"Not too good apparently, mind you she is ninety seven in a week's time, it's a big age. She has a cold at the moment and they're worried that it might turn into something worse. I told her all about your Rossano impersonation. She wonders how you knew".

"She talks a bit louder than she realises". Tony replied. "I agree, remind me to have a look in the mirror later. Anyway I want to pop to my place, see if everything's okay. By the way, I've decided to sell it. I can't be bothered with the hassle of letting. It would need a complete refurbish. At our age we might as well use the money to enjoy the rest of our lives".

"While we're at your house take a copy of those photos because Robert will want to take them to show Jane". Mary requested.

"What bothers me, is that Jane couldn't recognise Thomas from his photo, that's assuming he is their dad". Tony pondered.

"Well we know he definitely is their

dad. Robert's proved that with his bank statement. She was only seven and he was away working for weeks on end and here with me every couple of months, so she probably didn't see that much of him. I wonder if she'll know who the photos are".

"I'd be interested to see your family tree if you get round to doing one, it would certainly give you some new ideas to weave a story into a book when you get round to it". Tony muttered.

"I've already written seven chapters, just got a bit of a block at the moment. I wasn't going to say anything till it was finished, but now you're here for good It wouldn't be a secret for long". Mary replied. "Well let's get going, can we give my car a run ?" She added.

Robert burst through the hall like a greyhound out of a trap at first sight of the hare, leaving Mary and Gillian floundering in the doorway. "He's drove like a madman all the way to get here, I hope he's not going to be disappointed". Gillian retorted.

Tony handed Robert the two pictures and the grubby envelope. Robert immediately dropped in to a kitchen chair holding a photograph in each hand. "These were in this envelope ?" He stated answering himself.

"It seems to me that it was a waxed

envelope, or the photos wouldn't be in such good condition". Tony suggested.

Robert sat comparing the two images. "She looks older in this picture, but it's definitely the same woman". He stated. "But if this is my mum, who are the two babies she's holding. I assume one would be Jane....who's the other baby ?"

"Oh my God Robert, she's lovely looking". Gillian exclaimed leaning on his shoulders as Robert reversed the photographs to reveal the inscription on the back.

"Be careful what you're saying young lady". Mary snorted, part in anger and part in jest.

"What do you think about this picture ?" Robert asked referring to the woman with the babies.

"Well it looks like a hospital photo, and I think we're all thinking the same, one is Jane and the other is her twin sister. Your sister !. They both look like girls" Tony spouted. "That looks like a photographer's stamp on the back. And the hospital is probably in Fort Victoria. That's what's on the envelope". He added.

"It's got to be my mum". Robert cried, convincing himself as tears began to trace across his cheeks. "What do I do now ?" He stuttered.

"The obvious thing is to show them

to Jane, she should know if it is your mum". Mary advised.

Robert dried his eyes and continued to stare intently at the pictures for several minutes and then remarked that he wanted to be with Jane when she saw them, and wasn't going to send them by email. "Can I have these to take with us to Italy?" He pleaded.

"Of course you can, they belong to you more than anyone else, I've took copies for us so you take the originals". Tony replied.

"Now .... you're not going to run off, I've got dinner in the oven". Mary insisted.

"What time are you setting off to watch the lads play this afternoon?" Mary asked.

"Thomas managed to squeeze me in on the team coach, he's picking me and Robert up at twelve. And he's dropping Elaine off here, so you can have a good old natter all afternoon".

"You've not got long, it's twenty past eleven". Mary commented.

"It's as well it's next weekend they go to Italy, Robert desperately wanted to play today. It's the Three Counties Cup final, and it's the first time a team from a league as low as theirs has ever got to the final.

That sounds like his car". Tony remarked.

With the menfolk now en route to Truro for the afternoon and most of the evening, Mary and Elaine settled down in an armchair each in front of the log glow effect electric fire. Elaine in possession of the two copies of the photographs found in Thomas's leather folder.

"Tom told me all about his dad's things turning up, has Jane seen them yet ?" Elaine asked.

"No, Robert wanted to be with her when she sees them, he's got the originals, they're copies Tony took. They're off to Italy next Friday". Mary replied.

"I'll say one thing, your family is a complex one. Thomas is dad to my Tom, Daniel, Robert, Jane and possibly a twin sister to Jane. And you're mum to Tom, Daniel and Gillian. Have you attempted a family tree yet ?". Elaine joked.

"I've thought about it". Mary quipped.

After spending the afternoon in front of the television watching a film and having a late evening meal, the two ladies relaxed back into their respective armchairs.

"How long have you three been back ?" Mary shrieked, at suddenly being disturbed from her nap by their combined laughter.

"We've just this second walked in".

Thomas replied and gently tapped his wife on the shoulder. "Wake up dreamer".

"I wasn't asleep.....was I ?" Elaine spouted embarrassingly.

"At least you both had your mouths shut, that doesn't happen very often". Tony joked.

"He'll pay for that when you've gone". Mary informed Elaine with a laugh. "There's some dinners on the worktop, give them a few minutes in the microwave, not that you deserve any after that remark". Mary said..

"You've not mentioned the match, I assume you lost then". Elaine shouted through the open door..

"Don't ask ... Six nil". Thomas shouted back. "But we were playing the winners of the first division, we play two leagues below them".

"We did well just to reach the final". Robert stated marching into the lounge and proudly parading his medal.

"Thanks for the meal Mary, I'm going to have to shoot off. Gillian will be back home by now, She's been with Maxine, they've been helping out in the village hall for some charity all day".

"We'll get going as well mum. I think that's my last match". Thomas moaned as he physically struggled standing from his chair and trying to walk. "I think I'll just watch the lads next season". He muttered as he hobbled to the front door.

"Right then, it's just me and you now Tony. Do you want to watch some telle' ?"

"Well to tell the truth, I'm ready for bed". Tony chipped.

+++++++++++

## Chapter Eighteen

Mary drew back the curtains and stared at the rivers of rainwater streaming down the window panes. "It's absolutely tipping it down". Mary announced.

"It's been raining all night, didn't you hear it hitting the windows ? You must have had a sound night's sleep". Tony remarked.

"They should be there by ten if their flight went on time, we should soon know if Jane says it's her mother. Gillian will ring us as soon as she knows". Mary gushed with anticipation.

"I wouldn't have wanted their drive up to Bristol at five this morning, not in this weather". Tony commented. "It must have been horrendous ...... Are you coming to my place to meet the estate agent ?" He added.

"No I'm going to stay and wait for Gillian to ring ..... I know it's daft, I've got my mobile but I'd sooner be here".

"He suggested three ninety five". Tony replied in answer to Mary's question.

"And are you okay with that, it's a lovely old house with a lot of land".

"Not really but the agent reckons it's a bit isolated and needs a lot of work. Anyway I just want to get rid of it now. I told him to put it on for four hundred and ten thousand".

"Gillian's not rung yet, do you think she's alright, you don't think they could have had an accident on the way to the airport ?" Mary asked woefully.

"Of course not, we would have heard by now if anything had happened. Give them chance to get there and settle in. She'll ring you, just relax". Tony urged and gave her a comforting hug.

"At last, this must be Gillian". Mary gasped as she leapt from the settee to pick up the telephone handset. "Thank goodness you've called, we were beginning to worry about you". Mary cried.

"We did have some problems, but we've got here. Our flight was delayed a couple of hours because of the high winds and this end the baggage handlers are on go slow. Anyway we're here". Gillian replied full of excitement.

"Well !" Mary exclaimed impatiently.

"Yes it is their mum, Jane's still holding the photos, she started crying the moment she saw them and she's upset now over the other baby".

"Does she think it could be her sister ?" Mary uttered.

"Yes, definitely, she's sure it is. So I know as soon as she's got over the shock she'll start trying to find out what happened to her. She's convinced herself the baby is a girl".

"And is Robert alright?" Mary asked.

"Oh, he's in tears with Jane, they're huddled together at the moment. I'll ring you again tomorrow mum. I think Jane is taking us to see Rome if this weather clears, It's still raining cats and dogs". Gillian moaned.

"It has stopped here now, it's still threatening though. Speak to you tomorrow then. Bye Gillian". Mary concluded.

"Oh well, now we're certain, the lady in the photos is definitely their mum". Tony chuntered having listened to the conversation on the hall telephone. "I know Jane's a bit upset, especially if she's wondering why her mum never told her she had a sister, and most possibly her twin. But she must be happy to have a picture of her mum. I know Robert is". He added.

"It's a bit late to start, I don't feel like cooking tonight, how about eating out. See if you can get a table at the Sea Spray, give them a ring". Mary requested.

"It's still bucketing down again here mum, looks like a day indoors. Gianni brought a magnifying glass home from his office last night and we can just about make out the telephone number for the photographic studio. Jane tried it but there's no signal, so we think when the country changed from Rhodesia to Zimbabwe they had to get out of the country, or they were kicked out. But she's now searching the internet". Gillian uttered.

"There is a name of the photographer with the telephone number, Fort V or something like that". Mary advised.

"That's what she's looking for in South Africa, the country next door. She's hoping they just moved across the border, if not she's got a hell of a search, that's if they've kept their name, and still in business".

"I'll let you get on with your holiday, keep me informed. I hope the weather gets better for you". Mary said hopefully.

"Your powers have stretched across the continent mum, it's actually stopped raining and believe it or not the sun is trying to shine. Thanks mum". Gillian joked as she ended the call.

"Gillian's just been on the phone". Mary stated as Tony appeared and stood creating his private paddling pool on the kitchen floor. "Is it still raining ?" She added.

"Very funny". Tony chirped as the water continued to drip from his clothes and his hair. "It wasn't too bad till I just left the sea front and then the heavens opened". Tony replied after returning from a visit to Daniel and Debra's corner shop".

"I hope you kept my paper dry". Mary again ribbed.

"Never mind your paper, where's my breakfast ?" Tony jibed in jest.

"Anyway what did Gillian have to say ?"

"Where's the milk ? That's the only thing I asked you to bring". Mary snapped despondently..

"She didn't say that". Tony retaliated, causing Mary to laugh and defusing an unusual bout of temper.

"Never mind, if it stops raining I'll pop round, I want to see how Debra is, and how my grandchild is coming on. And if it doesn't stop you can go back". Mary said and then proceeded to relay Gillian's call.

Late in the afternoon the weather relented, the rain finally ceased and the sun even made a brief appearance allowing Mary to visit her daughter-in-law.

"And how was Debra ?" Tony asked as Mary wafted a four pint plastic milk container under his nose.

"She's well, Daniel was in the shop, he's given up his part time job for this year to help Debra and look after the shop after the baby's born. Mind you, they could do with a few more customers, not a sole came in the shop all the time I was there. I don't expect Gillian to phone again tonight". Mary ended. "Put the telle' on". She sighed.

"Yes Gillian". Mary responded the instant the telephone rang. "Any news?"

"Jane can't find any company with the name on the photo anywhere in South Africa. What she's done at the moment is to email the CIPC, that's their equivalent of our Companies House, she's asked if there is a company by that name been dissolved or hopefully changed their name, and she's asked for the names of any past or present directors if any. But it's Sunday today so she's given up for now. We're now going to go off with Jane and Gianni to do some more site seeing". Gillian said and then paused for a moment.

"Did you manage to get out yesterday then, you said it had stopped raining?" Mary asked taking advantage of Gillian's hesitation.

"Yes, I was about to say, the sun came out and we went to the Trevi Fountain and threw some coins in. Not that I wished for a lover. Well that's what I told Robert. Then we saw the outside of the Colosseum, so that's where we're off to now, to go inside and throw Robert to the lions". Gillian joked. "Jane won't find anything now before tomorrow, if then, so I'll ring you then. Bye mum".

Monday came and went without any progress. Jane attempted to contact the hospital in Masvingo, what used to be Fort Victoria, assuming that was where the babies were born, due to the photographer's logo on the reverse side of the photograph. The response she received was short and of no help, being advised that after to the formation of Zimbabwe all documents were destroyed or taken away by the incumbent authorities. Jane's only hope now depended on finding a connection to the photographic studio.

"I don't think Jane stands any chance of finding out what happened to the other baby now, the only good thing that's come from Thomas's folder is that they now have a nice photo of their mother". Tony chuntered.
"Yes, Gillian said that Jane has taken the photos to a professional studio in Rome to have them cleaned up and enlarged. If anyone's looking for that wallet or folder, whatever you call it. It'll be on the bench in the garage, I can't stand it in the house. I'll ask the lads if they want it. And if they don't it's going in the bin. Go and

stick it in the garage out of my kitchen".
Mary carped venting her anger with every
word .

++++++++++

## Chapter Nineteen

"No news this morning?" Tony enquired as he returned from a visit to the estate agent's office.

"Gillian's not phoned yet, how did you get on?" Mary asked switching a question on to Tony.

"They've had two viewings, one has put in an offer, but that one can think again. Three sixty, fifty thousand less than the asking price. I'm willing to consider offers, but not that low. The agent suggested I should get a gardener in for a day or two to give it a bit more kerb appeal".

"Kerb appeal! The house is half a mile from the nearest road for goodness sake, but I do know what he means, it does look a bit Adams family from the front". Mary quipped.

"I've agreed to do that, the agent is sending one of the lads from their maintenance department to do something with it". Tony responded.

The first half an hour of the afternoon tea dance was continually interrupted by a few of their friends wishing to hear about Robert and Jane's search for information regarding their mother and the two babies.

"I'll be glad when we can get back to normal and enjoy the dancing, that's the second week in a row we've hardly danced". Mary moaned as she turned the key in the front door and excitedly grabbed the handset from the desk at the first sign of a ring.

"Hello mum, you're back then, I tried you earlier, guessed you were off dancing".

"We've just walked in, I can see the answer machine flashing, I assume that's you. Has Jane found out something ?" Mary replied in anticipation of some good news.

"Not about the babies, but I didn't tell you that we had a good look at that wedding photo, you remember the one with the unknown girl, the one I thought looked just like Jane. Well Jane mentioned it to the studio when she collected the photo enlargements and they asked her to email it to see what they could do and they've done a fantastic job. They've got rid of the shadowy image. I'm not going to say any more mum. Check your emails !" Gillian chortled bubbling with excitement.

"Come on Gillian.......what !". Mary screeched. "Tony have a look at my emails". She urged anxiously, listening to her daughter giggling at the other end of the telephone. "This must be Jane". Mary squawked immediately Tony held the computer for her to see the picture being displayed. "Oh my God Gillian, you're not saying this is the woman in the photo?"

"Yes it is mum. Jane and Robert are jumping around like scalded cats at the moment. It must be the other baby with their mum in the photo. Jane's twin sister".

Mary was lost for words for several seconds, staring at the picture. "What's Jane going to do now?" She asked.

"She's now trying to find a telephone number for the South African Companies House, she can't wait for a reply to her email. But at the moment she's not having much luck, they don't seem to give one. Anyway mum, that's enough excitement for now. I will ring you again if Jane finds anything. Bye for now".

Mary and Tony dropped onto the settee still staring in amazement at the computer screen. "One of us needs to make a cup of tea, I know I could do with one". Mary exclaimed forcing Tony back to his feet.

"How the hell they're ever going to find this girl God only knows. The only chance of seeing her is if she comes back. She obviously knew Robert at the wedding so it's more than likely she will turn up. But why did she vanish on their wedding day and it's now been quite a while. She's had plenty of time to have come back". Tony spouted emphatically.

"Well, there's no doubting that it is Jane's sister, it's certainly not a coincidence that she looks like her. In fact she's her double, an identical twin". Mary retorted.

"Daniel has just this minute phoned, Debra had a baby girl at twenty past eight this morning. He took her into hospital in Plymouth late last night". Mary gushed with excitement.

"Can we visit ?" Tony asked

"Daniel reckons, everything is fine and they expect to be home later today. He's going to let us know when they're home. I must give Gillian a ring".

Mary's patience began to waver as she waited for her daughter to answer her telephone. "Come on Gillian, where are you ?" She snapped before tossing the handset onto the kitchen table. "At last, where were you ?" Mary moaned when Gillian returned her missed call.

"Sorry mum, we were out on the terrace having breakfast, what's the matter ?"

"Nothing, wonderful news, Debra had a baby girl this morning and everything is perfect according to Daniel. She is in hospital but they're coming home later today.

I must dash now, need to buy them both a present".

"That's fantastic, I'll send her an email from us here, let me know when you've seen the baby. Do they have a name ?"

"It should be Juliet if they haven't changed their minds". Mary replied.

"Don't go yet Granny, I can sense you're anxious to go shopping". Gillian joked. "Jane had a reply to her email and they gave her a link to their files. So now she's going to search on the internet back to nineteen seventy six, hopefully to find some record of the photo company. I'll keep you informed".

"I'll give you Granny, that makes me feel a hundred. Bye for now". Mary quipped and ended the call.

Tony steered his Mercedes across the footpath to park on the private area in front of the corner shop. Mary grabbed a large carrier bag from the rear seats, and within a couple of seconds was round the other side of the building ringing the door bell. As soon as the door would open she bounded up the internal staircase to the flat above the shop leaving Tony still shuffling his car into position.

Later in the evening after Mary had spent almost an hour lovingly nursing baby

Juliet, Tony thoughtfully suggested it was time to leave. Reluctantly Mary laid Juliet down in her brand new cot. "If you want a baby sitter you know who to call". Mary said.

"Thank you for her lovely tiny silver bracelet and all these lovely baby clothes". Debra replied, grateful that Tony and Mary had decided to leave.

"Don't forget what you just offered mum, I might be giving you a ring in the middle of the night". Daniel quipped.

"Come on then Granny, it's time we let these three settle and have some rest". Tony chirped.

"That's the second time I've been called Granny today, I'll clobber him when we get home, I want to be a nan". Mary instructed as Daniel followed them outside to the Mercedes.

Fifteen minutes later Mary lifted the receiver from the desk the moment they arrived back home. "You have one new message". The answer machine announced. "I guess you're with Debra and the baby I'll call you in the morning". "End of message".. The machine concluded.

"No you don't". Tony remonstrated. "It's too late, wait till tomorrow".

"But she must have some news". Mary pleaded as Tony removed the handset from her grip..

"Gillian hasn't rung yet". Mary griped to Tony. "I'm going to ring her".

"Hello Gillian, you rang last night".

"I would have rung you back earlier but we got involved in some exciting research".

"Go on then...tell me". Mary butted in impatiently.

"Well, firstly Jane had no luck with finding anything about the photographer's, it seems they just vanished, or they could have located anywhere, even a different name. But she found the equivalent of our Citizens Advice, and explained exactly what she was looking for, and they suggested she searches for Reuters News Agency Archives. That's what Jane's been doing since five o'clock this morning and you'll never guess what she found out".

"What has she found out ?" Mary again jumped in as Gillian paused to cross chat with Jane.

"Mother ! If you stop interrupting I'll tell you. This is all on the internet, Jane will give you the details and you can have a search yourself later. Anyway ..... she searched for news about Fort Victoria from her birth time of July nineteen seventy six, and found extensive coverage of a new born baby being abducted from the hospital and with that same photo of the two babies with their mum". Gillian accepted another interruption from Mary and then carried explaining. "It says that a young woman was arrested for stealing the child and she told the police that she had been paid to do so by an American Diplomat. But it never came to trial because she mysteriously died in custody".

"Oh my God. What happened to the American. Did they ever catch him ?" Mary stammered.

"No, because she hadn't revealed his name, that's if she knew it. And I suppose he'd have had diplomatic immunity anyway. But their conclusion was that the baby had been abducted and smuggled into America". Gillian spouted angrily.

"And didn't anybody get arrested for the girl's murder, because that's obviously what it was to stop her giving evidence". Mary snarled.

"No, no one. It's just recorded as death by unknown cause. Obviously a cover up by people in high places. That's about it mum, now we know, but Jane's still no nearer finding her, but at least we know what happened".

"We know she's alive, she was at your wedding. She's probably somewhere in America. It's a big country and you don't know her name". Mary gulped with a heavy sigh. Daniel couldn't believe it when I told him. Now he's got a new baby daughter and a new sister. I haven't told Thomas yet".

"Jane will email you the web site". Gillian informed.

"Did you hear all that Tony, what do you make of it ?" Mary asked as the call ended.

++++++++++

.

# Chapter Twenty

"It's Gillian and Robert". Mary shouted to Tony as she opened the front door. "Where's your car ?"

"We've just dropped it off at the garage in town, it's only in for a service. We had a nice walk here along the sea front, that's something we don't do often enough. Bit chilly though, but made a lovely change". Gillian replied, warming her hands over a lighted gas ring. "We just called into the last of the guest houses in the back streets, but no one ever remembers seeing Jane's twin. They all admired the photo, but no luck". Gillian added despondently.

"Susan rang last night, she asked how her favourite niece was doing. It's a pity they couldn't get down here for Juliet's Christening. But she has already made Walter book a couple of weeks off from his job to be at yours at the end of the month. So you'd better be on time young lady". Mary chirped.

"I do hope I am on time, Jane and Gianni are planning to come and stay for a couple of weeks as well". Gillian chipped in.

"Anyway, go and sit in the lounge, I'll make a bit of lunch".

"I'll run you back to the garage when your car's ready. Have they given you a time?" Tony asked.

"They reckon it'll be about a couple of hours, but they're going to give us a ring". Robert replied.

***************

With all the immediate family and few friends gathered around the font in the tiny village church, the vicar gently poured tepid water over the forehead of baby Katherine.

Gillian selflessly and very carefully handed her new baby daughter to Mary. Mary proudly carried her second born granddaughter out of the church cuddling her inside a pure white silk shawl against the late autumn chill. The brilliance of the Christening shawl contrasted vividly against Mary's petrol blue fitted two piece suit, bought specially for the occasion.

"A grandmother twice in the same year". Mary chuckled out loud casting an affectionate gaze in Gillian's direction. After a few quick poses on the church steps for photographs, the party of sixteen strolled the short distance to the local public house and into the small reception room.

Mary took pride of place next to a cosy log fire in a comfortable armchair with Katherine cupped in one arm and six month old Juliet trying to wriggle free from the other.

"It's your turn next Elaine, that's all I wish for". Mary cried sympathetically.

"That's what me and Thomas want, one day we hope". Elaine replied sorrowfully.

Susan took command of the generous buffet, laid out with an assortment of salads, sandwiches and hot food to start. "Plates this end, cutlery and serviettes at the other end. Come on someone make a start!" She called out above the din.

"Oh hello". The pub landlord exclaimed from the other side of the bar as Jane and Gianni, along with Robert sat on bar stools with their glasses of champagne waiting to toast baby Katherine. Jane courteously returned the 'hello'. "How is your father?" He asked to her puzzlement.

"I'm sorry". Jane responded. "But my father died a long while ago. I think you must be mistaking me for someone else".

"But I could have sworn you stayed here the one night to attend a wedding. Then you had to suddenly dash away because your father had been taken ill. I am sorry, I'm obviously wrong, but the resemblance is uncanny". The landlord extolled.

The landlord's words resonated in Robert's brain. "Do you still have a record of this lady's booking?" He asked almost shaking with anticipation.

"Oh my God, do you think it could have been our sister?" Jane screeched. Jane's loud outburst encouraged Gillian and Daniel to join them at the bar waiting for the landlord to return with his book of customer reservations.

It took several minutes before the landlord turned the book in Jane's favour and pointed to a particular booking. Jane and Robert huddled side by side to read the name of the pub guest. "How do you know this is the person?" Robert asked as his chest pounded with excitement at noting the date of the reservation being the day prior to his and Gillian's wedding day.

"Well if you read on, I made a note of ordering the young lady a taxi. And I noted her reason for leaving after only the one night". The landlord explained. This girl was the image of you, I know it's been a while but I could never forget her face, she was so beautiful, she was the only guest at the time. She sat where you're sitting now and we chatted for ages, then she had a call on her mobile and asked me for the number for a cab. I said I'd phone for one and she dashed up to her room to grab her things". He added, while continuing to stare at Jane.

"The one place we never thought of,

our own local pub. I didn't know they took in guests". Robert shouted causing a stir in the room as the story began to circulate.

"Would you mind if we made a note of the name and address of this lady?" Jane urged excitedly and went on to spend the next ten minutes explaining the whole incredible story.

After listening to Jane and Robert both pleading and pouring out their hearts he relented and allowed Jane to copy the information from his reservation book.

"This information is meant to be confidential, so don't tell anyone where you obtained it. And the best of luck with your search". The landlord retorted, happily smiling in the knowledge that he may have helped Jane to find her twin sister.

Armed with this exciting information, Robert desperately wanted to start making enquiries. With the party dwindling on well past it's scheduled time, and sensing that her husband's impatience was beginning to become obvious Gillian discretely asked the landlord to politely remind everyone that the room was now available to the public. Robert was relieved that only Tony and Mary along with Susan and Walter accepted the offer to accompany them the few hundred yards to their home together with Jane and Gianni who were staying at the cottage. Mary finally released custody of Katherine, but only when Gillian insisted on feeding her.

Within minutes of entering the cottage Robert and Jane became engrossed in the computer. After a cup of tea and yet more food, Mary and Tony decided to leave them to their search.

"Let me know if you find anything". Mary shouted as the Mercedes moved slowly away and on down the unlit lane.

"You gave me a right old whack across the back of my head with that magazine". Susan complained with a laugh from her seat in the rear of the car. "All I suggested that if Gillian's next baby is a boy to call it after her dad".

"Yes I know, we all know I'm just as good looking and as charming as him, but I'm a true Cornish man, I'm not an Italian, and my name's not Rossanno. Antonio sounds okay". Tony replied to a barrage of friendly insults from Mary and Susan.

"I'm on Tony's side". Walter commented, creating some arm twisting and more laughter from the rear seats.

Despite all the childish distractions, Tony safely completed the six mile journey home. "Well I'm ready for bed, I don't know about anyone else". Tony groaned.

"It looks like Jane is going to have to

write a letter to that address, there's no response from the lady's mobile number". Gillian informed the moment Mary answered the telephone.

"Can't she find her any other way? I doubt if there's many other Louisa Aliscia Johanson's living in New York". Mary asked, prompting a suggestion.

"Jane just mentioned that, she's doing a search now. She's just said there's only one with that name come up in Manhattan in a list of company directors".

"Now what's she doing?" Mary said.

"I'll ring you back mum, Jane's put in a search now for her company's details. That should give her a contact number".

"We're off out in half an hour, Susan and Walter are coming with us to the tea dance. Your auntie Susan's all glammed up and raring to go, but your uncle Walter's not too excited". Mary chuckled, listening to her daughter's giggles.

"I think Walter did very well, I don't know what you're moaning at Susan". Mary chuntered. "He got round to a waltz with me". She added.

"He danced like a clockwork toy soldier, but at least we've got him dancing". Susan joked. "He's got as much rhythm as a plank of wood".

"I can hear you !" Walter shouted at his wife through the open doors into the kitchen.

"Oooops ....that's my chance of getting him to lessons out of the window". Susan laughed.

"I'll get that, I hope it's Gillian". Mary gushed as she beat Tony to the sideboard to retrieve the telephone.

"Hello mum, well she's found the company and it lists just the two directors, James Samuel Johanson and Louisa Aliscia Johanson".

"And does it give a telephone number ?" Mary interrupted.

"Yes, and the registered office, which is the same address as the home address. Jane dialled the number but the receptionist wouldn't give out any information about Louisa and said Mister Johanson was away on business and to ring back in a week's time. Jane's getting frustrated and there's nothing she can do now and they're meant to be going back home on Thursday. Still .. .....at least we're getting somewhere. Robert has just found their house on Google earth, it's more like a mansion, it's enormous". Gillian gushed.

"Come on then Fred Astaircase, let's get going". Susan shouted from the front passenger seat of their modest dark blue Ford Mondeo. "I'll ring you as soon as we get home. Let me know how Jane get's on with her search for her sister".

Tony and Mary shivered in the cold air until Walter had driven from sight.

"We need a better fire than this, and your central heating's not a lot of good either". Tony moaned as he entered the lounge. "Why don't we have the chimney opened up and have a real open fire ?" He suggested.

"Because I don't want to, I know who'd be having to light the fires and clean the bloody mess every time....Me !" Mary squawked. "So forget it". She added sharply.

+++++++++++

## Chapter Twenty One

Tony was surprised to see the blurred outline of Gillian standing the other side of the part glazed front door.

"You again". Tony laughed as he opened the door. "We were only at your cottage last night, is everything alright ?"

"Jane rang earlier this morning, not good news". Gillian announced sadly.

"Where's Robert ?" Mary shouted while, standing in the open kitchen doorway.

"He had to go to football, he didn't want to go, he was very upset. Thomas called to our place for him, he's going to drop him off here after the match". Gillian replied as tears appeared in the corners of her eyes.

"What's happened then ? Come and sit down by the fire". Mary uttered softly.

"Jane rang the office number in New York again last night. The receptions again refused to give any information about Louisa but eventually put her through to James Johanson".

"Well …. And what is the news that's not good ?" Mary urged anxiously.

"Jane said he was very reluctant to speak to her until she fully explained the situation and told him that she was certain that she was Louisa's twin sister. She had to email him the photo of their mother holding the two babies and one of herself with Gianni to prove it was a photo of Jane. He rang her straight back and said that Louisa knew she had a sister, but he was absolutely knocked out by seeing this".

"For goodness sake Gillian, what is this bad news you're on about ?" Mary butted in impatiently wanting to know.

"Well, Louisa was knocked over by a hit and run driver and ever since she has been in a clinic on a life support machine. She can see and hear but other than that she's totally paralysed".

"Oh my God, how terrible, the poor girl". Mary sighed. 'How long as she been like this ?"

"Have they caught the damn driver ?" Tony interrupted.

"It happened a couple of days after our wedding. Jane never said whether they got the driver". Gillian replied with her tears now flowing freely.

"We now know why she's not been in contact. Did her husband mention anything about her being at your wedding ? I assume he is her husband". Tony urged.

"Yes he is her husband. He told Jane that Louisa knew all about Robert but she hadn't been able to find out anything about her sister. He said she easily found Robert and about the wedding and she was hoping her sister would be there. He said she got nervous and she didn't want to impose and spoil the wedding day. She'd decided to leave the introduction for later. But she had said that she cheekily sneaked onto a photo so that when she did contact Robert she could point herself out". Gillian said and paused to pour herself a glass of water.

"That explains all that, but why did she have to dash back home ?. Mary enquired.

"Her husband had to phone her because her father had a massive heart attack, but unfortunately he died before she got home. And then unfortunately three days later she was hit by this car". Gillian answered.

"I don't understand, how did she know about Robert being her brother ?" Mary asked curiously.

"Apparently her father and his second wife had a nasty divorce, his first wife died when Louisa was only a year old and he remarried twenty years later". Gillian stopped abruptly as Mary interrupted..

"How long was Jane on the phone to America ?" Mary gasped. "And with you this morning.

"Well past midnight. Now please stop interrupting mum". Gillian snapped and continued.

"Louisa found out from her stepmother a couple of years ago how her father had had her abducted and that she was not adopted as she had always been told. That is what the divorce was all about. His second wife threatened to inform the police, but she never did". Gillian answered and stopped for another sip of water.

"And how long were you on the phone to Jane ?" Mary gasped taking advantage of her daughter's break.

"All morning, me and Robert had an extension each.

"And why would Louisa dash home ? Surely she must have detested her father for what he did to her". Tony suggested.

"No, apparently he'd been a fantastic father to her, he'd looked after her on his own for most of her life. She thought the world of him. It was only in the last couple of years she'd found out". Gillian replied. "I could write a book about this".

"Don't you even think about it, I'm doing that". Mary joked, lightening the mood. "Oh my goodness there's more, how do you remember all this ?". Mary exclaimed as Gillian began speaking again.

"Louisa had been told the name of her real mother and even the hospital she was taken from, so it didn't take too much searching by a professional genealogist to find out she'd died in hospital. The death certificate gave the address in Horsham. Mister Johanson said they easily traced Robert but never managed to find anything about Jane".

"So I suppose Louisa assumed that Robert and Jane grew up together and hoped to see her at the wedding. Now she'll never meet them". Mary concluded sorrowfully.

"Yes she will !" Gillian gushed with emotion. "Her husband is sending over plane tickets for Jane and Robert and me and Gianni to go and see her. He said that would make her dreams come true. And they have three children for Robert and Jane to meet". Gillian said and immediately burst into uncontrollable sobbing.

"I hope he's not expecting some sort of miracle when she sees Robert and Jane". Tony said hesitantly.

"No, I suggested that to Jane and she said he knows nothing can improve her condition". Gillian replied through her tears.

"Where's Katherine ?" Robert called out the moment he entered the lounge.

"It's all right, I left her with Maxine for the afternoon, she's perfectly fine". Gillian retorted..

"I assume Gillian's told all about Louisa".

Robert said sadly.

"Yes, it's a very sorry story, I feel very sad for you and Jane". Mary responded.

"I rang Daniel straight after the match, we'd love to meet her one day if it's at all possible". Thomas asked.

"You've more right to visit her than me, you're her brothers, you can go in my place, and I'm sure Gianni would let Daniel have his flight. We'd have to clear it with Louisa's husband first". Gillian selflessly proposed.

"No, definitely not, leave the arrangement as it is. We will get to see her shortly. Just send back lots of photos". Thomas replied.

Immediately after Christmas the two couples travelled to New York to meet Louisa and stayed with her husband, James in their luxurious home where they also met their three children.

During their stay Gillian sent numerous emails to Mary and her brothers Thomas and Daniel.

'No miracles mum, Louisa appeared to smile with her eyes when she saw Jane and Robert, it was all very emotional. We all managed to contain ourselves until we left Louisa's room and then we all cried".

A very moving picture emerged of Robert and Jane sat either side of the bed holding Louisa's hands when Mary opened the first of many attachments, followed by a happy family photograph of Louisa and James with their three children, two young boys and a slightly older girl. The girl looking the image of Jane at that age. And coincidently named Jane .

For the next decade Mary lead a near perfect idyllic life. She had four more grandchildren. Gillian had another girl and called her Mary, followed by a baby boy they named Stewart. Debra and Daniel had a second child, a baby boy they named Tony. Thomas and Elaine had resigned themselves to never having children but two years earlier, making Mary's dream come true, at the age of forty three Elaine had a baby boy and named him Thomas.

Except for the usual every day ills, Mary and Tony enjoyed good health and tea danced their way through the years. Mary completed her book, but with no prospect of it ever being published the script remains as just another file on her computer.

*************

After the heartbreak and tears of meeting Louisa, Jane and Robert together with Thomas and Daniel made several trips to New York over the following years until Louisa finally gave up on life seven years after their first visit.

*****************

Sadly and devastating Mary and Tony's perfect life together came to a crashing end three years later in early December, when Tony died just three short weeks after being diagnosed with bone cancer, making Mary a widow for the second time.

++++++++++

## Chapter Twenty Two

Mary sat motionless and nervous in her designated seat gazing out at the almost deserted platform. With everyone now all aboard she felt a slight shudder as the Eurostar began to move away from Saint Pancras railway station heading for the Kent coast. She looked sadly at the seat on the other side of the table, empty except for her coat and her day bag. Mary closed her eyes momentarily wishing that when she looked again Tony would appear sitting opposite her. She knew this couldn't happen but it gave her some degree of comfort just to dream just for a moment.

Tony, Mary's second husband whom she married on a St. Valentine's day in two thousand and eight after a twenty five year romance, both then aged sixty five, died shortly before Christmas. Mary made the very courageous decision to proceed with the pre-planned rail holiday in memory of Tony, hoping it would relieve her heartache and her loneliness. The train was now speeding through the open countryside as she glanced across the carriage compartment towards her fellow travellers wondering if she was going to regret her choice.

Mary hovered edgily amongst the rest of the party as they made their way to another platform and boarded the waiting train to leave Brussels and on to Cologne for the first overnight stop.

Alighting from the transfer coach and entering the hotel, Mary was relieved to see a large number of luggage items stacked in the reception area. After half an hour of useful informative talk by the tour manager, a rather stout but very pleasant man in his mid forties, the guests gradually disappeared to their respective rooms.

Mary waited for everyone else to leave before collecting the remaining wheelie type suitcase, and with the excessively large key fob held in one hand she dragged her luggage across the floor to the empty lift with the other, only to be accompanied by a smart young man dressed in light blue jacket and cream trousers. The young man smiled at Mary and as the lift opened at the appropriate floor, took hold of Mary's suitcase and followed her to her door.

"That's very kind of you, thankyou". Mary said embarrassingly and handed him two Euro coins.

Mary spent the spare hour before dinner exploring her room and carefully selecting her outfit for the evening. Her initial thoughts were to 'dress down' a little, not knowing the custom on such occasions or what to expect from the other guests.

"Oh what the hell, sod em' all". Mary muttered to herself as she unpacked her favourite navy blue dress and smoothed out the odd crease. Now fully adorned in the very stylish, flattering, slim fitting outfit with matching navy high heeled shoes and clutch bag she posed in front of the full length wardrobe door mirror. "Not bad for a seventy odd year old bird". She chuntered to herself. Not wanting to admit to her real age. 'I must stop talking to myself'. She thought as she closed her room door and dropped the key fob into her bag.

Mary nervously stared into the dining room from the reception area as she left the lift. She could see that the thirty or so members of her party were already seated at two large circular tables. She hesitated at the open door and noted two empty chairs at the far side of the furthest table. Feeling like a fish out of water she could sense her pulse pounding in her chest as she started to walk across the room, when a stranger's hand took her left arm and guided her to her seat and promptly sat in the other empty chair. An elderly couple in the adjacent seats immediately engaged Mary in conversation, preventing her from acknowledging the companion who'd escorted her safely across the floor.

After several minutes of interrogating

Mary, the couple turned their attention to an elderly couple seated further along the curve of the table.

Mary noticed two Euro coins had been placed in front of her as she turned to speak to the stranger.

"Ooh ..... you're the kind young man who carried my case". Mary said with a startled expression. "I'm ever so sorry, I mistook you for the hotel porter, how embarrassing".

"Don't worry about it, you weren't the only one. It must be my outfit". He replied politely.

"Well you do look very smart, are you travelling on your own?" Mary asked.

"Yes, I think we are the only two singles on this holiday". He answered with a courteous smile.

"Aren't you a bit young to be on this sort of trip with all us relics?" Mary joked to recommence the conversation in between courses.

"It's a working holiday for me, I work for a travel magazine and for my sins they send me out on these tours to write up a review. It's hard work but someone has to do it". He said mocking himself. "Anyway who says you're old, all these others are old, you look wonderful, you're not old". He repeated sincerely.

"My God, you are a charmer, flatter away. Are you married ?" Mary asked and immediately felt a twinge of embarrassment for asking such a question in her situation.

The young man realised that Mary wasn't being offensive and explaining, joked that he hadn't found the girl of his dreams.

"I'm Thomas, Tom if you like, Tom Horton". He whispered in Mary's left ear.

"You can call me Mary. Mary Pennel. My husband was a Cornish man". She replied, explaining the origin of her name.

With the evening meal all served and eaten, Mary and her new friend transferred to the lounge next door to be served with their coffee.

"How did you get to become a travel writer ?" Mary enquired.

"Oh, my parents own a publishing company and it's one of their clients, so I suppose it was a case of who you know that got me the job". Thomas replied. "I'm also trying to write a mystery about a beautiful lady on a rail tour, so if you recognise yourself if it gets published, it is you". He added with a laugh.

"I finished writing a story a couple of years ago, it's about two hundred pages". Mary said in a whisper so as not to be overheard.

Thomas leaned closer to Mary. "Is it

any good ?" He whispered back. Mary and her youthful companion began to laugh raising curious eyebrows amongst the other guests.

"Well I would say 'Yes' wouldn't I, but it's just lying on my laptop". Mary sighed and then began to excuse her reason for being an elderly woman holidaying alone. "My first husband was a Thomas, he was a war foreign correspondent, he was killed somewhere in Asia a good many years ago. I've got a son, Thomas as well, he's in his late forties now".

"So did you ever marry again ?" Thomas gingerly enquired, hoping he hadn't caused any upset to Mary..

"Yes ...... To Tony, but he died just before last Christmas, he'd already booked this holiday as an extra surprise present. So I thought it might do me some good, I'm not so sure now if I've made the right decision". Mary replied sorrowfully.

On this note the conversation stalled for some time as Thomas could see that Mary appeared to be upset. "I'll give you my email address and you can send me your script, I'll pass it to my parents to look at for you". Thomas chuntered in an attempt to restore Mary's spirit.

Mary rose to her feet and thanked Thomas for the lovely evening and wished him goodnight.

"Thank you for your company, I'll see you at breakfast". Thomas replied.

The next morning Mary searched the dining room, but there was no sign of her young friend. 'Is he avoiding me ?' Mary wondered. 'I am quite early'. She though to convince herself that he hadn't deserted her as she selected a couple of finger rolls and a yoghurt from the breakfast bar and sat at an empty table.

The dining room chatter began to increase as the rest of the party together with another group of English speaking tourists gradually filled the room. Several of her fellow touring companions wished her "good morning" as they passed by her table.

Mary felt more lonely as each guest passed by, and with no one wishing to join her, she was about to return to her room.

"Guten morgen young lady".

Mary looked surprised but delighted as the tall fair headed Thomas sat down beside her.

"Young lady ! .. for a young lad you've got some charm. I'm old enough to be your grandmother". Mary laughed.

"You look just as young and attractive first thing in a morning as you did last night". Thomas extolled with a sincere smile.

"My God, If I was only fifty years younger, I really do love to have your company but you don't have to pander to an old woman".

"You're not old!" Thomas repeated emphatically. "We're both travelling alone and I would be delighted to have such a lovely friendly companion. I hope you are okay with me?"

"I'm very happy to have a handsome man like you as my companion". Mary enthused

"Good! Now I think we ought to make a move, we're supposed to be outside reception at nine, I'll meet you there. Put your case outside your room". Thomas reminded.

Mary sat relaxing with the majority of her fellow passengers looking out from the first class Pullman carriage, shortly to leave Cologne en route to Lucerne, watching as Thomas and a couple of the youngest gentlemen energetically loaded the luggage on to the train from the porter's trolley.

Thomas entered the carriage carrying his light blue jacket and occupied the seat directly opposite to Mary. The train shook and then smoothly drew away from the station and was very soon racing through the German countryside.

"Are you feeling alright?" Thomas asked Mary. "You don't look too well, can I fetch you a glass of water?"

"No .... I'll be fine, I just feel a bit queasy, it's probably only the motion of the train, it'll pass". Mary uttered. "Stop fussing Thomas, you remind me of my daughter".

Thomas leaned back in his seat and watched Mary close her eyes and immediately start to shake and perspire. Thomas could see the distortion on Mary's face as a couple of age lines she'd cleverly disguised resurfaced.

Thomas and an elderly lady traveller seated in the adjacent seat instinctively approached Mary's chair. Thomas gently shook her arm. "Is she going to be okay?" He asked the mature lady, assuming she would know what to do.

"She looks pretty poorly, give John a shout".

The tour manager swiftly arrived from his seat at the rear of the compartment, and was quickly joined by two more party members to give assistance. "Mary ... Mary, wake up love". John urged with no sign of response. "I think to be on the safe side I'll arrange for an ambulance to meet the train in Lucerne".

The waiting ambulance standing in the station car park was visible from the train as it came to a rapid halt. Within moments two Swiss medical staff entered the train and were at Mary's side. Thomas attempted to explain her symptoms as they carried out a brief examination before carefully lifting Mary into a wheelchair.

"You seem to have struck up a good friendship with Mary, will you go with her and I'll arrange to pick you up from the hospital later ?" John requested of Thomas. Thomas collected his jacket and Mary's handbag and followed behind to the waiting ambulance.

It was getting very late when the tour manager arrived to collect Thomas. "Sorry about the time, how is she ?" John asked as they climbed into a taxi.

"They say it's a fever, but until they know what it is she's quarantined in an isolation ward. "I've given them my phone number". Thomas replied.

The warm morning sunshine greeted the group as they assembled outside the hotel before taking the short stroll to the lakeside terminus. "I'll catch you up later, I'm going to pop over to see Mary". Thomas shouted to the puzzlement of the party as they began boarding the boat.

After some confusion with the language dialect and a lengthy explanation, Thomas was informed that there wasn't any change in Mary's condition. His insistence to see her was denied, adding to his frustration. He felt helpless as all he was able to do was to leave a message for Mary telling her he had to move on the next day with the tour but he would contact the hospital every day. This he did for the rest of the eleven day alpine tour, but Mary's condition failed to improve and on the last night from a Paris hotel he was informed that she had been flown back to England for specialist treatment.

+++++++++++

## Chapter Twenty Three

Mary returned to her Cornish seaside home to recover after receiving four months of intensive medical attention in a Hertfordshire hospital. Her health steadily improving and now being cared for at home by the local visiting nurse and her daughter Gillian.

Gillian entered Mary's bedroom. "Oh good you're awake mum. There's a man down stairs asking to see you, his name's Thomas".

A vice like grip of fear instantly knotted Mary's chest as she drew a rapid intake of air. Her mouth suddenly went dry and her pulse rate almost doubled. Her mind flashed back to the last time she saw her husband leave from Plymouth railway station in 1983 and the vision of his leather folder laid on her kitchen table.

Gillian was completely oblivious to her mother's plight as she called from the landing. "Come on up".

Mary became more panic stricken and gripped with anxiety with each footstep she heard as he climbed the stairs. This was the moment she once dreamed of but now was dreading. Mary could hear Gillian whispering the other side of the bedroom door as it slowly opened.

"Guten morgan young lady". Greeted

the tall fair haired young man with a cheeky grin. Mary's lungs instantly deflated and her panic attack melted away with an enormous sigh of relief as the handsome stranger leaned across the bed and held both her hands and kissed her on both cheeks. At the same time leaving two Euro coins in the palm of her right hand.

"Are you alright mum, you look as if you've just seen a ghost ?" Gillian asked.

"Yes …. I am now, I just thought, Oh never mind. Yes I'm fine, just a surprise".

"What on earth are you doing here, it's absolutely wonderful to see you again. How did you find me ?" Mary gushed.

"I had to know how you were, I hope you don't mind but I peeked into your handbag and took your phone number when you were in the ambulance. I rang your home to let someone know what had happened to you and Gillian answered, and she has kept me informed".

"So you knew all along that Thomas was coming here today, this is the young man I was telling you about".

"Yes I know, Thomas rang me the day you were taken ill and we've been in contact ever since". Gillian replied with a girlish giggle.

"You might have warned me. I would have got dressed and put some make up on". Mary moaned, then opened her hand and looked at Thomas inquisitively.

"Those are the exact same two Euros you handed me when you mistook me for the hotel porter in Cologne. You left them on the dining table". Thomas said as Mary's fingers gripped the coins.

"I'll keep these safe as a memory of meeting you on a holiday I was never meant to have taken". Mary replied with a regretful sigh.

"I'm sorry, I'm going to have to dash off soon. Another gruelling tour to meet at Southampton this afternoon. Someone has to do it ". Thomas repeated. "But before I go I've got a small present for you".

Mary sat propped up in bed looking astonished as Thomas revealed a book that he had secretly concealed between his newspaper. Mary gazed in amazement at the cover picture of herself staring across a Swiss lake, set against a mellow backdrop. "But how ?" Mary gasped.

"I told Gillian that I'd asked for your manuscript, and she emailed it to me. My parent's publishing firm had it read, they liked it and edited it, and the cover was Gillian's design. And that's the very first copy. It's the one and only hardback, it will be printed as a paperback when it's published in a few weeks time". Thomas paused as he watched the tears of joy trickling down Mary's face as she turned a few pages. "I really must go, but we will meet again, Gillian has all my details".

Thomas again held both of Mary's hands and again kissed her on both cheeks and then followed Gillian out to his car. "Your mum's book should be in the shops in a couple of months time, I hope it does well. We'll give it a good push in our magazines. It's been lovely to meet you after all our conversations".

Gillian stood and watched Thomas's car disappear from view before returning to Mary's bedside to find her staring at the inside cover with tears streaming down her face. Mary handed her daughter the open book. "You must have told him this about your dad, read the wonderful dedication he's written, especially the last line, your dad's favourite song title. 'Till I waltz again with you".

Mary carefully laid the book on the bedside cabinet next to Tony's framed photograph together with the two Euro coins".

**The End**

Thank you for reading my story
I  hope  you found it interesting
and  enjoyable
I  would  be  very  pleased  to
receive  your  comments
You  can  review  this  book  on
Amazon  books

Yours  sincerely  t.a.wood


Current  book  titles  by  t.a.wood


**"Mary"**

**"Missis  Hooper"**

**"Two  Yellow  Dresses"**

**"Message  for  Linda"**

The cover picture is a dedication to the author's wife, Joan who sadly died in December 2021.

Back cover   Swanage pier.

Printed in Great Britain
by Amazon

31298435R00116